The Great Railroad Race

The Diary of Libby West

BY KRISTIANA GREGORY

Scholastic Inc. New York

Colorado Territory
Denver, 1868

May 2, 1868

I am being punished again and have been sent to the attic. I'm crushed that Mother is so angry with me, and unhappy about sitting up here alone.

That's why I welcomed the noise from outside. It sounded like a stagecoach was coming, for there were loud janglings of harnesses and many hooves. I threw open the window and leaned out to see better. Coming through the trees that shade our road was something I'd not seen before. Six mules were pulling a bright red wagon. I could read WELLS FARGO AND COMPANY in gold letters along its side.

When I saw Father leaning over the fence waving his hat in excitement, I forgot my misery. The driver parked in front of the wide-open doors of our barn. He was wearing a blue army cap (he must've been a Yankee like Father). First they shook hands, then began dragging two large crates from the back of the wagon.

Right away our horse, Tipsy, wandered over from her favorite spot under the apple tree. Father petted behind her ears, then slapped her rump so she'd get out of the way. Finally the driver saluted Father, climbed back up to his seat, and snapped the reins. As the wagon disappeared through the trees, Father threw his hat in the air and did a jig.

A jig! He must not have known I was watching. I have an unhappy feeling that when Mother comes home from the dress shop, she's going to be surprised about those crates. And mad.

This reminds me, the dress shop is why I'm here.

Early this morning Mother and I walked along Third Avenue. We saw a pretty bonnet in the shop's front window so we went in. There in front of the mirrors was Mrs. Cotton, standing in her corset and bloomers while being measured for a gown (she is quite large and bulgy). When she saw me she threw her arms out and cried, "Libby! Come here, darling."

She reached for my cheeks and pinched them hard, *very* hard. Then leaning close to me she asked, "Sweet child, how are you?"

I rubbed my cheeks and backed away from her hot breath. I'm fourteen years of age and do not like being pinched. "Ma'am," I said, "I feel like a horse just bit me."

I didn't mean to hurt Mrs. Cotton's feelings, for she is

a very dear friend of ours, but the way she straightened up and looked at me, then looked at Mother, I fear I did. Mother blushed with apologies, then hurried us both from the shop.

Mother said if I have thoughts that shouldn't be spoken I must *write* them instead of *saying* them out loud and making people feel bad.

"That's why we gave you this journal, Libby."

Two hours later

I'm still in the attic, writing on top of an old trunk. Except for this little milk stool to sit on, there is no furniture up here, just boxes and crates. Joe snuck upstairs with his sack of toy soldiers — to comfort me, he said — so I've been playing with him on the floor. He's a good brother, and he is a comfort, though he's only six years old. A few minutes ago Joe and I leaned out the window to look down at the garden. When we saw Father there, reading a newspaper, we whistled and drummed our hands on the sill until he heard us. I don't think he realized I was being punished because he smiled up at us and pointed to the mountains. Our "Rockies" are beautiful at this hour, purple in the fading light. Right now there are dark clouds over them and streaks of lightning. I hear thunder.

And Mother's calling my name. I'm forgiven! (Has she seen the crates? I wonder.)

May 3

Rained all day. I brushed my hair into a neat braid and curled my bangs with the hot iron so they came to the middle of my forehead. Then I put on my dress, the blue one with black piping along the waist and hem, buttoned up my shoes, and folded a clean hankie into my pocket. Now ready to go visiting, I sat at Father's desk in the parlor to write a note of apology to Mrs. Cotton, for I am truly sorry to have hurt her feelings.

Joe stood looking over my shoulder as I blew on the wet ink, and said he was sorry, too, even though he'd not done anything wrong. As I put on my cloak, he asked if he could please come, too. So, together he and I walked through the drizzle to her cottage — I held his hand so he wouldn't jump in puddles. Mrs. Cotton lives opposite us, on the other side of Roaring Creek, and often we wave hello to one another from our porches. Joe and I rapped the brass knocker twice. When she opened the door I was surprised that she seemed madder than yesterday.

"Your father should be shot," she said, holding up the morning's newspaper. Her lace collar cupped her chin like a doily, and her cheeks were flushed.

"Pardon?"

"That's right. You tell him I said so." She pressed the paper into my hand, then slammed the door. Joe looked up at me.

"Don't worry," I told him. "It's probably just another one of Papa's articles." I took the envelope from my pocket and pushed it under Mrs. Cotton's door so she might find my note later. As we walked back across the bridge I thought, Why do people get mad at *me* for what my father writes? He's a reporter for the *Rocky Mountain News*, and even though his name isn't on his stories or editorials, Denver is a small town, so folks know what meetings he goes to.

Mother was rolling pie dough when we came in the back door. She wears her hair loose, bundled into a net that falls to her shoulders. When she smiles at us, I think she's the most beautiful mother on earth.

Joe leaned his elbows on the table. "Mama," he said, "Mrs. Cotton said she's gonna shoot Pa."

Mother sighed. "What is it this time, Libby?"

I read the article out loud. She put her hand over her mouth to keep from laughing. Flour covered her cheeks. Since she's so cheerful, I'm *sure* she hasn't been out to the barn yet. Mother says the barn is Father's business and the kitchen is hers.

Next day

About Father's article. He had attended the Literary Society Tea hosted by the governor and several big so-and-so's. Father reported that the meeting was — these were his words — *boring, utterly boring . . . another useless gathering of windbags who stuffed themselves on cookies and punch while pretending to understand literature.*

At least when I write things that aren't nice my words are private — one thing I think I'll love about this diary. I love it already because Father sewed these pages together with his own hands, from blank newsprint. That's why the edges are uneven. He cut the paper himself. Mother pasted in one of her ribbons for a book-mark, then covered the front and back with calico left over from her last dress. It's a pretty diary. (My birthday was three weeks ago, but I keep forgetting to write in it.)

I wonder if fourteen is too old to start a good habit.

May 6

Well, it happened. Mother went out to the barn.

All morning she'd been busy about the house, opening windows for fresh air and hanging our comforters outside. I was on the back porch sweeping when I saw her come out of the chicken coop with eggs gathered in her apron. She passed in front of the barn and, to my surprise, let out a frightful scream.

I dropped the broom and ran. Joe came, too, and even Tipsy trotted over from the pasture to see what she could see.

Mother stared into the barn, hands on her hips, the eggs in broken puddles at her feet. "What is it and why is it here?" she asked.

Father took off his hat to wipe his brow and tried to smile at her. When he described what was in one of the crates and that it only cost $165, Mother turned on her heel. She stormed off down the road to Aunt Lil's.

Now it is my own mother who is furious at Father. She wasn't back by sundown, so I tied an apron over my dress and set the table. Then I sliced some cold ham and bread, put out a plate of pickles, and filled the pitcher with milk. I didn't dare try cooking something from scratch because usually I burn things.

Joe asked about 20 times, "When will Mama come back?" but throughout supper Father only spoke once.

"Please pass the butter, Libby."

I lay in bed for hours it seemed, watching the moonlight move shadows through my little room. As I am in the southwest corner of the house there are two windows, one in each wall. At night after blowing out the candle I open the curtains to see outside. I love to watch stars in the black sky.

It felt lonely knowing Mother was not home and I wondered if Father also was awake. I hope she comes back soon. She's never left us like this, ever. I pressed my face into my pillow so no one would hear me cry.

May 8

Almost midnight. My candle is low, so I'll try to write quickly, for much has happened these last two days.

Mother stayed at Aunt Lil's all that night. When she came home the next morning, she hugged Joe and me and kissed us again and again. She said she was so terribly sorry to have left us and promised she would never, ever do it again. Then she unbuttoned her sleeves to roll them up, put coffee on the stove, and pointed the sugar spoon at Father.

She said, "Sterling, we are going with you. That's final!"

He put his hands in the air and said, "All right, Julia, whatever you say." At that, Joe jumped off his stool and yelled, "Hooray!"

About the crates. Inside one was a Washington Hand Printing Press. It stands on little iron legs, is about two feet tall, and weighs 700 pounds. The other crate has equipment such as buckets of black ink, an ink roller, paper, wooden trays, and boxes of type. These boxes are full of letters from *A* to *Z*, which will spell out words and sentences, and the letters are all sizes, the smallest could almost sit on the head of a pin, and the largest fit in my palm. It seems Father and his army friend Pete (they were in the war together) plan to publish their own newspaper!

About Pete. I don't know him well for he's quiet when he comes around. Pinned to his vest is a thin silver chain attached to a silver pocket watch that he often checks for the correct time. After he announces that it's two o'clock or whatever the time is, he then closes the lid with a neat click and slips the watch back into his pocket. Another thing about Pete, I've seen him sitting in the shade with a book, but what he reads I don't know.

Back to the newspaper. Pete and Father told us they're going to travel with the builders of the new transcontinental railroad (I can't say this word without stopping twice — it means going across the continent). They said a railroad company from California, Central Pacific, and one from Nebraska, Union Pacific, will meet somewhere in the middle of the American desert.

"It's the Great Race, Julia," Father told her, "the story of the century. When and where the two will meet, only God Almighty knows, but Pete and I plan to be there to write about it."

He said they'll stay in tent cities that follow the newly laid tracks. In between printing a newspaper, Father will telegraph the news to Denver — he'll be what is called a "stringer," someone who writes eyewitness reports. (I wonder if this is because the telegraph wire looks like a string?)

Must go. Joe is calling me. . . .

Later

About Father. During the war he was a combat telegrapher in Pennsylvania. He would send and receive military secrets. He told me he knows things that would make my hair curl.

Father loves news and he loves danger. I think he's tired of writing about tea parties, and the Great Race is much too exciting to pass up.

May 10

Joe and I are in the attic again, but not because we're in trouble. Mother has been talking to Father all afternoon about his adventure, but now she's very upset. Whenever her voice gets loud, Father closes the parlor windows so the neighbors won't hear, and we hide upstairs. I don't mind her being mad, we just don't want her to leave us again.

"It's too dangerous for a family," he is telling her. "Julia, there are drunks, thieves, and murderers, shootings every day." He says that Indians are so mad about the railroad disturbing their land that they've been ripping up tracks and cutting down telegraph wires; they've even attacked and scalped some of the surveyors.

I guess Father has changed his mind about us coming with him.

I know one reason Mother is unhappy. When the war ended three years ago, she was so surprised and thrilled that Father came home alive she vowed they'd never again live apart. He and Pete had been prisoners together in the Andersonville prison camp. It was a miserable, cruel place. Many, many Union soldiers died there, from terrible wounds and disease and from not enough food to eat. Now Father gets sick easily and sometimes his legs ache so bad he can't walk. Mother says she wants to be near him, to care for him.

Well, last October she went with him on a business trip. (Mrs. Cotton came to stay with Joe and me.) The trip was called the Editorial Rocky Mountain Excursion. Two hundred journalists, including Father and Pete, were invited by the Union Pacific Railroad to see the newest tracks. They went to Julesburg, Nebraska, and watched workers at the end of the line inch forward rail by rail. There were banquets and band music on board, buffalo shoots and a Wild West show with friendly

Indians, everything to make reporters write nice things about the railroad moving west.

And they did.

Newspapers across America, even some in Europe, printed stories that said emigrants will be able to travel the continent in just a few days instead of months on a wagon train.

I remember one article. It said, *The more people who move West, the more rainfall.* Also, *Steam from locomotives moistens and enriches the soil.* Mother said those words were just lies from men who want to make money selling land.

Same as the lies men told about gold. I think Mother is still mad about that. In 1859, when I was just five years old and Joe wasn't even thought up yet, we were living in the city of New York. When Father was thirteen years old he was a printer's apprentice for the *New York Tribune.* Later, he wrote stories about politics for the newspaper.

Well, his editor was an adventurous man named Horace Greeley who kept telling Father and his friends to "Go west, young man, go west." Mr. Greeley took his own advice. When he was in Denver and saw with his own eyes that there was gold to be mined, he sent reports back East. Father, who is also an adventurer, hurried up and moved us out West, to the territory of Colorado. There were plenty of folks who got rich at Pikes Peak, but not Father. He lost every penny we had. (I think Mother is also mad at Mr. Greeley.)

Father painted a sign on the back of our wagon that said, PIKES PEAK AND BUSTED, then moved us up here to Denver and took a job setting type for the *Rocky Mountain News*. Father worked there a couple years, then joined the Yankees and went to war. While he was gone Mother took in boarders who loved her cooking and were happy to pay 50 cents a meal. (I wish I had inherited her talent for cooking.)

Back to the gold. Father says he doesn't care anymore about being a millionaire because it makes life complicated and besides, we can't take one cent of it to heaven. His favorite saying is, "God brought us into this world with nothing but our birthday suits and that's how we'll go out."

I don't know. Right now I don't care. Mother is crying and Father has ridden off on his horse. I can hear hooves galloping down the road. Joe has laid his head in my lap.

"Is Father leaving us now, too?" he asked before

falling asleep. I stroked his forehead and said, "Don't worry, Father will return soon." But to myself I wished they could have a disagreement without one of them storming away.

I'm too upset to write any more.

After supper

Rain and wind beat against my windows. Trying to race the cold I quickly changed into my nightgown and wool socks, then hung my dress on the peg behind my door. Went to Joe's little room and turned down the covers on his bed, then brought him to the kitchen where it's warm. He likes to eat a cracker dipped in milk before going to sleep.

Mother was in her chair by the fire. She had taken her hair out of the net and was brushing it over her shoulder, something she does every night before she goes to bed. Her hair is a beautiful reddish-brown and is wavy from being tucked up all day. Father says she and I look alike and that my hair is just as pretty, but I don't know. Our looking glass is as small as a pie tin, so I'm not sure what my whole self looks like.

I've put a kettle of water on the stove to make Mother

a nice hot cup of tea — maybe this will cheer her up, for Father is at Pete's cabin tonight. I wish he were home.

May 12

Father did return. On the way home he rode by the postmaster's to pick up our mail, which included a letter from Mr. Greeley, for they write each other every six months or so. At supper when Father had finished his soup and pushed aside his bowl, he put on his eye-glasses to read the letter. Mr. Greeley said that a railroad to the Pacific will be America's greatest achievement.

Sterling, the letter said, *get the story.*

When Mother heard that Mr. Greeley is partly behind Father wanting to follow the Union Pacific, she stood up from the table and went to the window. She propped it open to let in the night breeze. "First it was Pikes Peak," she said. "I just hope for our family's sake that Mr. Greeley is right this time."

After supper I went into the attic to wrap a present for Joe because tomorrow is his birthday. He's been admir-ing my dominoes and the little oak box they're stored in. I carved his name, *Joe West*, on the lid so he'll know it is really his now.

Joe turned seven today. Mother and I made a chocolate cake, four layers, with whipped cream. No little candles because I left them too near the stove and they melted. When he opened my dominoes he let out a happy yell and began playing with them right away.

"Thanks, Libby, thanks," he said.

Mother and Father's gift to Joe was an interesting one, a book about a real-life adventure at sea called *Two Years Before the Mast*, by Richard Henry Dana, Jr. The chapters have a lot of big words and very long sentences. I thought it would be too difficult for him to read, but my brother is stubborn.

At this moment he's sitting near the hearth in Mother's rocker, reading it out loud to her as she kneads bread dough on the table. She is smiling at the way he slowly pronounces each word. Now Father has put down the newspaper he was reading to gaze at the fire, his eyeglasses pushed back on his head. I know he's remembering his own adventures aboard a sailing ship.

Finally when Joe had closed his book Father began the tale he's told us many times. "I was just a lad of ten," he said, "a cabin boy out of New York Harbor, aboard the brig *Clementine.*" How I love to hear Father's stories. It's no wonder he wants to hurry off to watch the great railroad being built. While he dreamily talked on, Mother sliced the cake and served us.

Later, after they both tucked Joe into bed, I washed our plates in a pan of hot, soapy water, then dried them with my skirt — I was in a hurry and didn't want to search the cupboard for a new towel. Of course, I would never do this if guests were here.

Well, when I was done I sat in the parlor to read the newspaper. (It is one of the few late-night privileges I have that Joe doesn't.) One headline said that an editor in Missouri was tarred and feathered for something he said about the mayor. Another editor, this one was in Ohio, was horsewhipped on the steps of the courthouse for a story he wrote about the sheriff. When Mother came in from the privy, I read the stories to her. Now she's more determined than ever not to let Father go off alone with Pete and their printing press.

"In case he writes something really stupid," she told me.

═══ ═══

A telegram arrived for Father. The Western Union boy who delivered it lives across the creek — I know him from Sunday school — well, he held out his palm until Father realized he wanted a tip. But finding no coins in his pocket Father instead shook hands with him and said, "There's a good lad."

That's just like Father. His dreams are big, but he often forgets little things like where he's put his money or his eyeglasses.

The telegram was from the Freeman brothers, two Johnny Rebs he met on the Editorial trip last October. These brothers also have a Washington Hand Printing Press and have started a newspaper called the *Frontier Index*. They're making lots of money from advertising and are beating other papers with the news as they follow the railroad crews. *See you on the railhead,* they wrote.

"Well," Father said, "now that the war's over, I don't mind fighting these boys with words instead of bullets." He turned to Mother and said, "Time's a-wasting. I've got to go."

She put down her knitting. "We," she said.

"All right, Julia. We."

Mother had won. I'm happy she's brave enough to keep us together.

May 16

Tomorrow we go with Father and Pete to Cheyenne. Union Pacific has built a station there and is sending little trains west with supplies for the work crews. Aunt Lil will see that our house is rented while we're gone, maybe a year! But I don't want to be gone for a year.

What about Annie and Kate? They're my best friends. And when I'm gone, who will sleep in my bed? If I find out it's an old snoring man, I will weep. Something else — I just sewed, with my own needle and yarn, the curtains hanging from our wide kitchen window. They are yellow with lace edges and so pretty. My favorite time of day is morning when sunlight comes through and makes patterns on the table. I don't want a big slurping man to sit here in my spot in my chair looking at my curtains. What if he has a sour wife who won't sweep the floor or empty the mousetraps? Our dear home will become a shambles!

I'm just miserable about this — if Mother heard me say these things she'd think I'm selfish. But I can't help it.

During our trip Mother will be schooling Joe and me with arithmetic and other such. He thinks this will be fun because he doesn't like school, but I do. I'll miss my friends, I'll even miss Mrs. Cotton, because every Tuesday she takes us older girls to her house for etiquette and afternoon tea — that is where I learned how to serve sugar cubes with tiny silver tongs. Also, she taught us that when setting the table there's a proper way to strike a match against sandpaper without knocking down the candles.

Everything is a mad dash, so I'll hurry. Trunks to pack with clothes and cooking things, also our big, old dictionary and Bible. From Denver we'll head north by wagon and will be able to rest at Camp Collins. People call it a fort, but there are no walls for protection, just a guardhouse with soldiers. Father told us not to worry, though, he's sure we'll be safe from Indians.

+═ ═+

May 23
Cheyenne, Dakota Territory

It's been a week, but here we are. One of our oldest mules died on the way, it just dropped dead in the road. Father and Pete dragged it to a ditch and rolled it in. Then two hours later the wagon's rear wheel split in half. So Mother and I unloaded our cooking box, Joe found rocks to make a fire pit, then he gathered twigs and such. We spread blankets in the grass. Nearby was a creek and oh, it felt good to take off our shoes! The water was so cold our feet quickly grew numb so we'd lie in the sun for a while, then go wading again. I lifted my skirt to my knees, but Mother said it's all right among family. (Pete was sleeping in the shade of the wagon so he didn't see.)

When Father came to tell us the wheel was fixed, he took off his hat and scooped it into the shallows to have a drink. He looked up at the clouds — tall, white clouds in a perfect blue sky. He smiled at Mother and said, "Pretty place to camp, Julia."

We stayed two nights!

Father was in such a hurry to leave Denver, but in no such hurry to leave our nice spot by the creek. I guess he's the type of adventurer who also likes to lie down in the grass and stare up at the sky. I love this about my father.

Later

Cheyenne looks bare compared to Denver. Father said it's a brand-new town because of the railroad. The main street has thin little trees planted in front of the hitching rails. There are too many saloons to count, a few cafes, at least two newspaper buildings, a jail, and a blacksmith. Someone said they're building a schoolhouse and a theater so civilized people will move here.

I miss Annie and Kate. Before I left they invited me to a proper tea in Annie's front parlor. We dressed in our best white dresses, I wore my new little white gloves that cover my wrists, and we practiced our manners. Kate likes to end her sentences with "dear," such as, "Would you care for some cream and sugar, dear?"

My favorite thing to say is, "I'll have a bit more marmalade, please." That day we promised one another never to be unkind and gossip, something we like to do.

But no sooner had we made this promise when

Annie's neighbor, Mrs. Pendergast, swished into the hallway without knocking on the front door. Without saying "hello" or "I beg your pardon" (for we were at that moment pouring our tea), she made an announcement. With her arms spread wide and in a high voice she said, "Horace and I are having dinner with Governor Cummings, tra la, tra la."

Our mouths were open, but no words came. She bent over our little table and helped herself to three butter cookies, dipped them into the strawberry jam, and ate them, in between licking her fingers. I was horrified. Before we knew what to say, she was gone.

Early the next morning we left on our journey so Annie, Kate, and I barely had a moment to whisper about Mrs. Pendergast.

I'm glad I have a diary to put down these happenings, but sometimes I do enjoy gossip, even if it isn't polite. (I want to know how a lady with wretched manners was invited to dine with the governor.)

May 24

Mother, Joe, and I are staying upstairs at the Cheyenne House. (Father and Pete are camping.) The walls to our room are not really walls — they're just sheets hanging from a rope and since the sheets are only flour sacks sewn together, we can hear every single word people are saying. *Everything.* An oil lamp hanging in the hallway makes our walls glow with light and shadows. Last night when we were in bed, I saw the silhouette of a man taking off his shirt and scratching under his arms. Mother said, "Libby, turn your eyes."

For privacy she first blows out our little candle before taking off her net and brushing her hair. She says there's only one man alive who may set eyes on her before bed, and that is Father.

Noises are worse. The first night I couldn't sleep. There were so many men snoring, it sounded as if we were riding a locomotive. Other sounds, too, that Mother says a lady shouldn't mention.

But I'm not a lady! I'm a girl writing in my diary. Well, last night a man made a shocking noise that sounded like a trumpet blast. There also is belching and spitting. Cursing, too. It's a dreadful place.

I'm sitting on our bed, writing this by the light of the tall window. Joe is next to me reading his book. I can see down to the train tracks, just in front of the hotel. Men are busy loading flatcars with lumber, iron rails, and other supplies for the builders. Two barrels that have the word WATER painted on their sides are on one flatcar, and there's a boy about my age sitting between them. I wonder if he's one of the children hired to carry drinks to the workers.

One of Cheyenne's newspapers, the *State Tribune*, has a daily column called "Last Night's Shootings." Mother's face got pale when she read this, but she was silent. She worked too hard to get Father to take us — I know she won't complain now. But she makes sure that we eat supper early, in the cafe downstairs, and are in bed before dark. I don't know which is noisier, this hotel or all the saloons that stay open until dawn.

It's almost summer, but it's cold enough that I've been wearing wool leggings under my dress. I'm tired of them — they prickle! Speaking of fashion (ha!), Joe has started tucking his trousers inside the tops of his boots because he saw one of the railroad men do it. And when he's trying to think of something to say he now squints and looks at the sky, then hooks his thumb under his suspender with a loud snap, just like the telegraph operator does.

I think Joe looks silly, but don't want to hurt his feelings, so shall leave those words here.

Later

I've been getting mixed up when I hear people talk about the two railroad companies, so I invented a trick to help me remember which is which.

Union Pacific starts with a *U* and is building its tracks westward, alongside us, and "us" begins with *U*. The other part is this: Central Pacific starts with a *C* and it's coming from California, which also begins with a *C*, and most of its workers are Chinese, another *C*.

When I told Joe, he laughed and said, "Clever girl!" with a snap of his suspenders. Maybe it's not so very clever, but it will help me remember, as the Great Race presses on.

Next morning
Still in Cheyenne

A few days ago Father and Pete loaded the printing press and everything else onto their wagon and hauled it to the next railroad town, Laramie. It's about 50 miles west. They'll set up their newspaper office in a tent, then send for us as soon as there are cots and a cooking stove.

In the morning before they left there was a mad

search for Father's eyeglasses, which *I* found in his shirt pocket when I leaned against his chest to hug him. At this, Pete opened his watch and held it into the sunlight to read the time.

"Well," Pete said, "six-fifteen, we better get going." He clicked it shut, put it into his vest, then tipping his hat toward Mother, he climbed onto the wagon seat.

At breakfast, the hotel clerk brought Mother a copy of the *Frontier Index*, the Freeman brothers' paper. They are with the Union Pacific crew somewhere in Wyoming. While Mother read this aloud to us, I was also listening to three men at the next table who were talking with excited voices.

"If our boys don't hurry," one of them said, "we're going to lose to old Crocker and his Pets."

I leaned closer to listen. While the men cracked open their soft-boiled eggs and dipped toast in the yolks, they kept talking. It seems Crocker is one of California's rich railroad bosses and his "Pets" are the Chinese workers, hundreds and hundreds of them working hard and fast and for pennies a day.

Now I know two things.

Even though I've never seen Chinese men with my own eyes, I think they wouldn't like to know they're being called Pets. The other thing. Men with beards and open chewing mouths should *not* eat gooey eggs without a napkin tucked under their chins.

May 26

A telegram arrived for Mother. It said, *Julia, stay in Cheyenne two more weeks. Don't worry. Sterling.*

Mother picked up her purse and marched downstairs. Joe and I looked out the window to see her walking to the train station (as fast as a proper lady can), holding her hat down against the wind. A few minutes later she was back with three tickets to Laramie.

"Two weeks, my foot," she said.

I do admire Mother's gumption.

May 27

We packed our bags early and stood on the platform. It was cold and windy. When we heard the train whistle and saw a huge cloud of steam rising from the smokestack, I felt a thrill. Mother did, too, because she squeezed my hand.

On the train we sat on hard benches and stared out

the windows. As it pulled up a steep grade, it slowed down and chugged up and up. The hills looked bare as we climbed in altitude. Then at the top of Sherman Summit we stopped. A whoosh of steam flew by our window and even though the engine stood still for ten minutes it continued to make this sound: *ch . . . ch . . . ch . . . ch . . .*

Some buildings lined one side of the tracks, a store, a few saloons. A conductor leaned over our seat to lift open our window. Cold, cold air came in. He pointed. Far in the distance was the snowy mountain of Pikes Peak (where Father did not find gold), then westward was Longs Peak.

But Joe didn't care about mountains. All he wanted to know was why did we stop and why was this summit called Sherman.

"Well, sonny," the man said. He took off his cap and put it on Joe's mop of brown hair. "This town is more than eight thousand feet above sea level and since William Tecumseh Sherman was the tallest general in the Union Army, someone thought to name this place after him." The conductor said this is the highest elevation station in the world and that we had stopped to bring folks supplies.

We watched as men unloaded barrels and crates

from one of the boxcars. I noticed a tent next door to one of the saloons. A sign hanging from the doorway said, DAILY JOURNAL. In front there were two men sitting on a log, smoking pipes. I guess there isn't much news at Sherman Summit.

May 28
Laramie City

It's dark out and Mother has sent a messenger to look for Father.

We're now at the Laramie Hotel. It was built just two weeks ago and is noisier than Cheyenne House, but its dining room is elegant — polished silverware and china, starched white tablecloths, and kerosene chandeliers. The wood floors shine.

Anyway we barely arrived here *alive* — I've never had such a fright. Leaving Sherman Summit I looked out our windows, and as the train snaked downhill I watched the cars that were hooked up behind us. Railroad men were standing on the roofs — in the cold, blowing wind — turning handles so that below them the brakes would squeeze against the wheels and slow the train down.

My heart pounded. What if the brakemen fell, or the wind blew them off? Gradually the train did slow down, but still I was afraid. The worst was yet to come, though.

Some miles west of Sherman we came to Dale Creek and that's all it is, a creek, hardly any water. But its canyon walls are so wide and tall Union Pacific had to build a bridge.

The train slowed down almost to a stop and we looked out our windows to see why. Mother gasped and put her hand to her throat. Ahead of us was a wooden trestle so high up and frail-looking it seemed as if it had been built with toothpicks and string.

As the engine pulled forward, ever so slowly, I noticed the ground had dropped away on both sides of us. The bridge was so narrow, if I were to stick my hand out the window to drop a penny it would fall down and down and down to the rocks. When a gust of wind made our car sway, passengers screamed, myself included. Mother pulled Joe to her, she was so frightened our car would tip over.

Finally we made it across, only one quarter of a mile, but it felt like ten. Later when the conductor explained that Union Pacific hauled the timber bridge in sections from Michigan, then built it in just 30 days (that's why it was so wobbly), Mother looked at him with her mouth open.

"But, isn't that dangerous?"

"Oh, yes, ma'am, but we're in a hurry. Once we meet up with Central Pacific our boys will come back and re-do it. Most of the bridges are like this."

Mother leaned back on the bench and took a deep breath. "Oh, my," she said.

The hotel is busy tonight — there's piano music downstairs and the clink of glass as someone washes dishes. I'm not at all sleepy, but Mother says it's time to blow out the candle. No word yet from Father. I hope he's all right.

June 1

Looks like we'll be staying at the Laramie Hotel for a while. We found Father and the reason he wanted us to wait was because his tent caught on fire and is now just a lean-to protecting the press, no cots or stove.

The fire started when some men shooting at each other missed. No one was killed that night, but a bullet cut the rope where Father's lantern was hanging. It fell and kerosene spread fire up the tent walls before he and

Pete were able to beat it out with blankets. Oh, I'm thankful the bullets missed them and that they weren't burned.

He was proud to show us his first issue, printed two days ago. It's just one page with big headlines about UP crews now being near the border of Utah Territory, maybe 200 miles from here. He gets his news, he said, from the work train, which has its own telegraph office. Someone there taps messages to the office here in Laramie, where journalists wait to copy down the words. They in turn pay the operator to telegraph a story to their newspapers in Chicago or wherever.

For example, Father showed me a telegram with just seven words:*TEMP BRIDGE GREEN RIVER MASONS BY WINTER*. Father turned these few words into dozens by writing that Union Pacific crews had completed a temporary bridge over Green River in Dakota Territory and that by Christmas, masons would be laying stone and mortar for a permanent bridge, so on and so forth.

I asked him if he ever makes mistakes by guessing at the in-between words.

"Sometimes," he said. "But I try to make my stories as truthful and accurate as possible. That's why they say newspaper reporters are writing the first rough draft of history."

So, that's how it's done if someone wants stories fast. Otherwise editors must wait days for mail to reach them by stagecoach because there are no more Pony Express riders — they stopped delivering news seven years ago. That's when telegraph wires were finally connected coast to coast. Personally, I don't understand how clicking sounds coming over a tiny copper wire can spell words, but those sounds obviously make sense to some folks.

Father's little paper looks good. He's called it the *Daily West*, but it's not daily, and it's not as fancy as the *Rocky Mountain News*, but so what? There are two columns of advertising; saloon owners and store merchants here pay him 20 cents for each word! He's also making money by printing business cards. Just for fun (and to make Mother happy), Father made up an ad — it's almost half a column long — for her older brother, Henry, who lives in Salt Lake City. Because the railroad might go through there and workers might need supplies from Henry's store, Father said this advertisement could bring Henry some new customers.

Father was wearing his best red suspenders, a blue

shirt, and his hair was freshly combed when he pointed this out to Mother. I think he looks like a real editor, though he has misplaced his eyeglasses again.

Later

More about Pete. He mainly sets type and runs the press, but he's untidy — I mean he looks lonely, as if no one has cared for him in a long time. His shirt is stained and smells bad. His beard needs to be combed, too — there are bread crumbs and yellow specks that I think are dried egg yolk. If it weren't for his silver pocket watch I would guess he's never owned a nice thing in his life.

But Pete is kind to us, and every time he sees Mother he tips his hat and lowers his head with respect. He calls her Mrs. West, not Julia, and he calls me Miss Libby. Sometimes he calls my brother "Sonny Joe."

When I complained to Mother about Pete needing a bath, she said, "Don't you worry about Pete. In the prison camp he gave up his own blanket to keep Father warm when Father was dying of pneumonia. Pete can stink to high heaven for all I care. He saved your father's life, Libby."

I hope I can be nice to him, but for now I think I must breathe through my mouth when he comes near.

June 5

Pete taught Joe all the verses to "John Brown's Body" so now Joe sings it over and over and over. He wouldn't stop so I pinched his leg hard, then hid my hand inside my dress when he started screaming. Mother marched me downstairs, holding my arm tight, and whispered, "Young lady, we'll have none of that."

We were standing on the stairway that goes into the lobby. Two ladies passed us, their satin dresses brushing against ours and they smiled at Mother but turned scolding eyes upon me. I was embarrassed and mad. Joe never gets in trouble for anything.

I'm alone on our bed. Mother has taken Joe down to the dining room for a piece of hot apple pie, probably with whipped cream on top. He always gets what he wants.

I wish we were back in Denver. I don't like the rough men or this hotel and I've changed my mind about Mother being brave. She's just selfish for wanting to be near Father.

Sunday, June 7

Mother took us to church. It's really a general store, but there were chairs and stools lined up like pews on the dirt floor. The preacher stood behind a counter. I don't know about anyone else, but all I could look at was the jars and jars of candy — butterscotch, licorice, peppermint sticks, and chocolates wrapped in wax paper. Joe swung his legs until Mother put her hand on his knee. Three boys about my age sat behind me. I know, because one of them kept pulling my braid, and when I turned around all three of them pretended to be praying.

I wanted to slap them, but decided doing so would only land *me* in trouble.

Later

Father and Pete are now at Fort Sanders, not far from Laramie. In a few days we'll have a wagon man drive us there. Mother says, "Tent or no tent."

I guess we'll be safe from Indians. All the stories I've heard about them so far are just stories because I've not seen one with my own eyes.

A locomotive heading west with two cars and a caboose stopped for thirty minutes so its passengers could eat dinner in the Laramie Hotel. It was a hurry-up affair, but I saw General Sherman with my own eyes! And he is tall. He wore a white vest with a bow tie, and a coat that hung below his knees. With him was another general who has been nominated for president of the United States, Ulysses S. Grant. Mother said he's campaigning, but she has a low opinion of politicians because they don't seem to care that ladies aren't allowed to vote. When the generals left, I noticed their tablecloth had been stained with tomato soup and some gelatin had fallen to the floor. (General Grant also left the stub of his cigar in his teacup.)

This reminds me of my farewell party in Denver and the rudeness of Mrs. Pendergast. I guess that just because someone is high society or in politics doesn't mean that person is well mannered.

This afternoon a steam engine — *No. 23* — pulled up to the station. It had deer antlers on its headlight! In front of the cab was a steam dome that was so polished some men combed their beards while looking at their reflections. It was a handsome train but the antlers made it look ridiculous.

Laramie has a roundhouse. It looks like a huge, round barn with stalls, enough for 20 engines to be fixed if they need fixing, for there's also a machine shop and blacksmith. Joe and I stood outside where we could see into one of the wide doorways.

Soon we heard a whistle and saw a train arriving from the East, a noisy, chugging engine with clouds of steam. It was switched onto a sidetrack to get out of the way, in case another train should come from behind or from the opposite direction. While it was on the side-track some men unhooked the engine from its coal car, its boxcars, and caboose, then signaled the engineer.

He drove very slowly into the barn, onto what looked like a giant dinner plate, then with a loud burst of steam the locomotive came to a stop. Now the plate began to turn, like the slow ticking of a clock. When it finally stopped, the engine was pointing in another direction and was ready to drive into one of the stalls for a check-up. Or onto tracks heading back from where it came.

Watching with us was an elderly man with a long white beard (it was tucked into the top of his pants). He said that this roundhouse was built with stones hauled here from Rock Creek about 50 miles away. He also said that someday Laramie will be a real city because of the railroad.

"The Great Race is going to put this town on the map," he told us. "Just wait and see, yessir."

June 10

I've met a girl whose father is one of the surveyors. Ellie Rowe is her name and she is staying with her mother down the hall from us. Oddly enough they, too, live in Denver!

Ellie's dress is the latest fashion, a plaid skirt that comes below the knees, then big, ruffled bloomers that go to her ankles. Her boots are calfskin, black, and they squeak when she walks. I want to make friends with her, for she is cheerful and smart. When she saw Joe reading *Two Years Before the Mast*, she asked him what he thought of the ship's voyage around Cape Horn. It's one of her favorite books!

Last night before bed Mother told me about Ellie's house in Denver. It's a mansion with a carriage house and servants' quarters, built with money Mr. Rowe made during the gold rush. But I don't care. Even if Ellie is rich, she acts like a good, regular girl.

June 11
Still in Laramie

A terrible thing has happened.

Joe and I saw a boy killed today. He was about ten years old and was standing in the middle of the tracks. When an engine came around the bend, it blew its whistle over and over until he jumped out of the way.

But what only a few of us knew was that he had just put a copper penny on one of the rails to see if the train would squish it flat.

When the train passed in front of the station, its heavy iron wheels hit the penny and spit it toward the boy, striking him in the forehead. He fell to the gravel. The way his left leg twitched we thought he was playing, but then he stopped moving. His mother ran over and scooped him up in her arms. I myself start crying at the memory of her terrible screams.

Our own mother came running, others did, too, to find their children. A telegraph man hurried outside.

He waved his arms to shoo everyone away from the tracks.

"Never, never put coins on a rail!" he cried. Then he explained that the rails are rounded at the edges, not flat, so when the train wheels hit, a coin can shoot out like a bullet instead of being run over.

We're all so sad for the boy's family. He was just having fun.

The next day I caught Joe kneeling by the tracks. He had just put a penny on the rail and was waiting for an engine to run over it. I couldn't believe it. My own brother! Doesn't he understand?

I picked up a stick to whip him, but thought to myself, he'll just cry and Mother will think I'm being mean again. So I took his hand and kept him with me until I found her in the hotel parlor. She was reading her favorite magazine, *Harper's Weekly: A Journal of Civilization*. Instead of whipping him as I would have, she put down her magazine, gave him one hard swat on his bottom, then spoke in her angry voice. He was so brokenhearted, he wouldn't eat supper and he just cried himself to sleep.

Mother worries about Father, now I worry about Joe. Being near the railroad is more dangerous than I thought. Is being part of the Great Race worth my brother being hurt or — a horrible thought — killed?

June 12

It is sunny and warm — I took off my leggings and folded them into my little trunk with cedar chips. These will keep moths from eating the wool.

To cheer up Joe, I took him with me to meet Ellie. We walked along the tracks, she in her squeaky boots, all of us singing, "John Brown's Body." There are surveyors here who are laying out parcels of land so people can build houses and stores. Ellie said that she once saw her father's maps and if we were birds flying over Laramie, the town would look like a checkerboard.

Each block equals one square mile, the same as 160 acres. Somehow the government manages all this land and is allowing every other square for the railroad, and letting homesteaders have the ones in between. This way the railroad won't be able to hog all the land. Regular folks can live here, too.

Mother has a bad cold, so we will wait a few more days before going to Fort Sanders. She's in bed with a fever, so I'm in charge of Joe. I will try to be patient and kind, but sometimes I'm short-tempered.

I'm anxious to catch up to Father. I want to see with my own eyes how this railroad is being built (and how exactly is he publishing his own newspaper?). I also want to see a Chinese man. Another thing, if there really are Indians out there, even if they're mad at white folks, I want to see them. Since I'm just a girl, will they be mad at me, too? Oh, there's so much I want to learn, things I've not even thought of yet. I wish the days would go faster!

We heard another rumor this morning that the Californians are making better progress than we are! People in the hotel are talking fast and furious about this.

Later

We ate supper in the dining room with Ellie and her mother, a fine lady with the manners of a queen. When Joe dropped his buttered bread, face-down, on the pure-white tablecloth I hurried to wipe it up, but only made a dark smear. Mrs. Rowe just smiled and said, "Never mind, dear, there are waiters to clean up."

Joe and I carefully, slowly, carried a bowl of chowder up to Mother, but forgot the spoon. So, Joe made a lot of noise running downstairs to fetch one and when he came back, not with a soup spoon, but with a tiny little one from the sugar server, I held my breath for wanting to scold.

But his smile was so proud I said, "Joe, you're a good boy."

He was tired so before bed I read to him from his sailing book, just two pages. Thus we fell asleep without a fight.

June 13

Mother is worse. Her fever makes her pillow wet. Mrs. Rowe is tending her. I wasn't worried until I saw a man in a black coat hurry upstairs carrying a black bag. A doctor! Later Mrs. Rowe came to me.

"Libby," she said, "I think it best if you and Joe sleep in our room for a while."

Her words frightened me. How sick *is* Mother? I know I must be brave, but how do I take care of Joe and should I send for Father?

June 15

A thunderstorm with lightning has kept Joe and me inside all afternoon. There are other children, too, and we played leapfrog in between the dining tables. The chef came out in his apron and tall white hat, clapping his hands, yelling, "No, no, no! Get out, you stinking brats!"

There is nothing to do while waiting for Mother to get well, for she just wants to sleep. I'm tired of trying to keep Joe out of trouble. After breakfast he knocked over a water pitcher that had been left on one of the tables. (It made a fearsome crash.) The other children ran and hid, except Ellie and Joe — he cried and cried, he was so sorry.

Ellie helped me sweep up the broken glass and mop the floor while a hotel clerk made sure we did it right. He stood the whole time with his hands on his hips, looking at us — my cheeks burned I was so embarrassed.

Joe isn't naughty on purpose. I think the problem is that he's a boy.

Before bed

My heart is heavy. Joe is asleep beside me in the trundle we fixed next to Ellie's. Mrs. Rowe has spent all day with Mother and is silent with fatigue.

"Everything's going to be all right," I whisper to Joe. I'm trying to be cheerful for him, but I'm upset. When he had fallen asleep I crept into Mother's room. She was breathing hard and her eyes were open, but when I spoke she didn't answer. I mopped her brow with my handkerchief and smoothed back her damp hair.

"Good night, Mother," I whispered, kissing her cheek, then quietly I left.

June 20

Three days of no rest and much worry.

Last night I couldn't stand to be away from Mother any longer, so I lay in a blanket on the floor next to her. Whenever she stirred I reached up to hold her limp hand and talk to her. At least 20 times I said, "I love you, Mother." At least 20 times I thought, *Please don't leave us.*

June 21

Up and down the stairs all day it seems, with a pitcher for Mother, for drinks and sponge baths. I haven't spoken aloud of my worry, so must write it here. She seems weaker with each passing day, oh God!

June 22

In a panic this morning I ran out across the railroad tracks, far into the sagebrush where no one could see me. I wept and wept. What if Mother dies? What will become of us? I can't think straight to write about other things.

June 23

I collapsed at breakfast, just slipped from my chair to the floor like a rag doll, Ellie told me. A man carried me upstairs to the trundle where I've slept most of the day. Mrs. Rowe says it's exhaustion and nerves and that I *must* rest and stay composed. But how can I with Mother so ill?

I'm feeling calmer today. But when I saw that Mother was still silent and drawn, my heart sank. Will I know how to be brave if she dies?

Ellie has been such a dear friend to me during all this. Each night before bed she brushes my hair one hundred strokes and chatters gaily, telling me not to worry. She gave me one of her nightcaps, a pretty thing with a lace hood and blue ribbon to tie under my chin.

Then every morning Ellie takes Joe for a long, long walk along the railroad tracks and makes sure he has no pennies with him and doesn't cause mischief. In the afternoons she sits with him in the downstairs parlor, playing dominoes and helping him read his book. I peeked at them once from the hallway. She was scolding him for something, pointing her finger. I could see that his chin was quivering, but he stayed in the window seat like a brave little gentleman. I was amazed. If ever I scold Joe, we get into a fight and he accuses me of bossing him around.

Now about Mrs. Rowe. She treats Joe and me as if we were her own children, never bothering us with her worries. When not at Mother's side, Mrs. Rowe is with us. She makes sure that we sit together at each meal and practice our please-and-thank-yous.

"Joe, dear," she says, "tell us some more about your book. What are the sailors doing now?" She waits patiently while Joe fidgets, then suddenly remembers and begins telling his version of the story. Then it's my turn, then Ellie's. By the time dessert arrives we are all deep in conversation.

Mrs. Rowe is helping me to be strong by keeping my mind active and showing us how to care for one another. I'm grateful to her and hope she and Ellie will stay with us for the rest of our journey.

June 25

My neck and shoulders are stiff. All this day I sat in a chair by Mother's bed, worrying, watching, praying. She reminds me of a quiet, frail bird struggling for life. I fear I must get word to Father somehow, but if I'm too late will he ever forgive me?

June 26

Joe is tucked into the trundle sound asleep, and I'm downstairs in the lobby writing quickly by the light of a little desk lamp. Mother stirred this afternoon when I put a spoon of broth to her lips. She whispered my name . . . dare I hope she'll live?

June 27

Today, oh joy, Mother sat up in bed. She is as pale as this paper, her voice barely a whisper, but she is smiling. My dear Mother.

June 30
Fort Sanders

Mother rested for three days. Now that she's alert we've traveled to Fort Sanders. Father was so happy to see us, but he asked why Mother is so weak and pale. She doesn't want to upset him so she said she'd had a slight cold.

Well, Father and Pete changed the name of their paper to *The Weekly West* — it's too much work to publish more often than that. Father said it takes them at least three days just to pick out all the little letters from their boxes and arrange them to spell words, sentences, and paragraphs. Then when the paper is printed, he and Pete must put back each little letter into its proper box so it'll be there the next time. Father said that the circulation for each issue is about 45 copies, or until the ink runs dry on the press.

Fort Sanders is a busy place. Corrals with horses, soldiers marching here and there. Two blacksmiths work all day hammering iron for chains, tools, wagon wheels, all sorts of things.

Outside the fort there are many tents, mostly belonging to families of railroad workers. Some wives have set up big boiling pots to do laundry, others cook all day with meat turning on a spit. Now that we're not staying at hotels we are back to fixing our meals, a chore I dislike because I usually boil, bake, or fry things too long or not long enough.

In the distance, I can see a large herd of cows grazing. They belong to Union Pacific and every day some are butchered to provide fresh meat, others are used for milking. Men on horseback rope them with the help of several little dogs that run circles around the cows to keep them together. A sharp, short whistle from a cow-boy is the only thing telling these smart dogs what to do and when. At night I can hear guitars and wonderful music. Father said the men sing lullabies to their cattle; they also write poems.

I think cowboys must be tenderhearted to do such lovely things.

Well, rumors about the Great Race confuse me. Before breakfast a man in a wagon rode through camp yelling, "Hooray, we're winning!" Then just a few minutes ago Father read us a telegram that said Crocker's Pets have pulled ahead by miles.

I don't know what to believe.

Later

The campsite we share with Mrs. Rowe and Ellie is set back from the tracks, far enough away so gravel doesn't spit out in our direction when a train runs by, but close enough that the ground shakes when it does. Our family now has a cozy tent, a cot for Mother and me, and pallets on the dirt floor for Father and Joe. And Pete.

I'm holding my tongue and shall put my unkind

words here instead of speaking them. Pete snores and he still has not bathed or combed his beard. And when he leaves in the morning for the newspaper office (still a lean-to), Mother rolls up the back side of our tent, then opens the front to air things out.

If she has angry thoughts she keeps them to herself.

In front, by the doorway, we've put two milking stools so Joe and I can sit and watch the world go by. To shade our little porch, Father made an awning from a piece of canvas. When my chores are done I like to sit here with a newspaper. (There are lots of stories on one page and it is easier to hold than a book!)

Two papers I read today have curious names. One is called *The Babbling Bumblebee*, the other is *We Don't Know So Don't Bother Us*. Most interesting, though, is that both newspapers were *handwritten* on one side of a piece of paper. Father said circulation is six or seven, or until the editor's hand gets tired of writing. When I was done reading I passed both pages to Mrs. Rowe, who also laughed at the names and said she'll pass the papers on to the next person.

In one of them she noticed a small article about a clipper ship sinking off the coast of New Jersey, so she read it aloud to Joe. He leaned into her arm and stared off into the distance. "Do you think there were any cabin boys on board the ship?" he asked her.

A telegram arrived today for Mrs. Rowe from her husband. She sank onto our bench with relief after reading that he is well but missing his family.

July 1

I've wondered about the various trains passing by, going west. If the tracks end somewhere in the territory of Utah, how do the engines turn around to come back this way since there are no roundhouses yet?

By the way, we bought a mule for 25 cents. Its owner was so mad at it for refusing to budge, he threw up his hands and yelled, "Two bits for a stupid mule!" Pete and Father have had no problem with it. In fact, the mule seems happy to be with our other three.

Pete came to the supper table with a gallon jar of lemonade he'd purchased from the fort. It had slices of lemon floating on top and had been sweetened with honey. He was so proud to ladle it out into our cups that I must admit his cheerfulness touched me.

Still in Fort Sanders. I should be paying better attention to the correct date, but even Father gets mixed up. Today his newspaper said, *Juno dS*. I think he meant to print *June 25* but somehow got the letters and numbers mixed up. No wonder. I tried to pick some out of their boxes, but because everything is backwards, they're easy to misread. The letter *S* looks like the number 5 and *o* looks like *e*. While I was trying to help, Pete called over from where he was working the press.

"Miss Libby," he said, "be sure to mind your p's and q's." I didn't know what he meant until I peered into the boxes and saw how much those two letters look alike, especially with ink smudged on them.

Father's front page news: Crocker's Pets are pushing across the Nevada desert. One of Crocker's big boss friends, Leland Stanford, took a stagecoach from San Francisco all the way to Salt Lake City to meet with Brigham Young, who's president of the Mormons.

When I came to this part of Father's story, my mind drifted far, far away. I've heard Mr. Young has a dozen wives and so many children he can't remember their names — this is all I could think of for an hour. I even made up a poem. It's not very good, but here it is:

> *Old Brigham Young lives in twelve houses*
> *With too many children*
> *and too many spouses.*

The Great Railroad Race is interesting but I think Mormons are more so.

Later

For breakfast Mother cooked flapjacks on our little stove while I set our table. It's an upside-down crate with wide cracks (sometimes the forks fall through). She and I *wish* we could spread our nice cloth over it, but the other day Pete used it to wipe off the ink roller. I thought Mother would choke when he told her. So we are just careful where we lay our spoons and such.

Our plans have changed a bit. Instead of staying with the railroad workers, we ladies and Joe will winter in Salt Lake City. This way when heavy snows set in we'll be in civilization, not stranded in the middle of nowhere. Also, we'll be able to visit Uncle Henry and my cousins.

I'm happy to have a girl my age to talk to. At night before bed Ellie and I go into her tent for some good whispering. First she brushes out my hair, then I brush hers. She wants to be an actress because she's good at swooning. This is how she does it: She throws her arm in the air, tilts her head back, bends her knees, and gracefully crumples to the ground, making sure her nightgown covers her ankles. She can do this six times in a row.

"Actresses don't flop," she said out of breath. "And Libby, always keep your knees together."

I hadn't considered being an actress before, and even though it does look like fun, I think I'd rather write a play than be in one.

Something else Ellie and I whisper about is men who have many wives. I guess this is gossiping, but we agreed that when we get to Salt Lake City we would have to make the acquaintance of a Mormon girl and ask her some questions — some very *personal* questions.

After all, Mr. Horace Greeley himself interviewed Brigham Young. It seems right that a girl such as myself could interview a Mormon girl. This is *my* opinion any-way.

Later

During the day Ellie wears her hair in two pigtails, tied in back always with a ribbon to match her dress — today it is red-and-green plaid. She also knows how to multiply 9s and 12s very quickly. If we were in school together I think she would be Teacher's Pet. To look at her sitting prim with a book in her lap, you'd never guess she can swoon in dramatic style.

This afternoon we invited her and her mother for tea, three o'clock. I swept the dirt in front of our tent so it looks nice, and we set everything up where we had a pleasant view. The prairie stretches as far as we can see, and towering above the horizon are fluffy white clouds. Father calls the sky se-roo-lee-an blue, but when I asked how it's spelled he didn't know. He puzzled over this for several moments, then asked Mother. She opened our dictionary and began flipping through the pages. "C-e-r-u-l-e-a-n," she read. "Same color as your eyes, Libby."

"Yes," Father said. "Beautiful, beautiful blue."

About Tea Time. If Mrs. Rowe noticed our bare table she was too polite to mention it. Mother filled our china pot with boiling water and let the leaves steep while I set out saucers and cups. We baked corn muffins to serve with butter and jam, but just after I set things down a gust of wind blew dirt across the table! Sand stuck to the butter, it was in our sugar and every bite of muffin. For once I didn't burn anything, yet things were still ruined — I was so upset.

Ellie saw my despair and quickly said, "I do say, Libby, the ladies in Boston aren't having as grand a time as we are."

"No indeed," said Mrs. Rowe. She winked at me, then nodded toward Joe. He had pulled his napkin from his shirt and was flicking it toward a passing cat. Thankfully, the cat ran away in time. Oh, I wish I had a sister! I wish *Ellie* were my real sister!

During tea I asked Father again why the railroad companies are in such a hurry. He lit his pipe and thought for a long while — he hadn't seemed to notice the sand in his tea.

"Libby," he finally said, "the world revolves around money." He said the reason why Union Pacific and Central Pacific are racing each other is because the government is loaning them between $16,000 and $48,000 for each mile of track they lay. These loans can be repaid later at a very small interest rate.

Now I understand. The more track, the more money they'll be able to borrow. The more they borrow, the more they can invest and so on.

Later

Joe says he wants to be a water boy. Father said, "Yes," but Mother said, "Absolutely, positively no. Over-my-dead-body, no." It would be too dangerous for him to be among the workers, she said. Busy men don't know how to keep little boys out of mischief.

I met a photographer today. He has a little wagon with black wooden sides. I forgot to mention him before, but he has been traveling alongside us, taking pictures of bridges and trains and workers, to document everything for Union Pacific. His name is Mr. A. J. Russell. His camera looks like a large bread box and sits on a tripod. When he looks through his viewfinder, he pulls a black tarp over his head to keep out the light. Everyone must stand perfectly still until it's over, because otherwise they just show up as a blur when the photograph is finished, that's what Mr. Russell said.

There are other men taking pictures, too. Union Pacific has its own little steam engine that pulls a "Photograph Car," no caboose. A sign painted on its side says, STEREOSCOPIC & LANDSCAPE VIEWS OF NOTABLE POINTS. It passed by a few days ago, heading west. When it blew its whistle, people looked up from whatever they were doing and cheered. The car was painted bright yellow with red lettering and was decorated on top with a pair of elk antlers.

Antlers again — ridiculous!

About this Great Race. Even if the railroad bosses are just doing it for money, I still think it's grand. I want to see who wins, although we only hear rumors about who's ahead. Someday I myself want to ride the train coast to coast.

On another subject, several days ago Pete made a checkerboard. He found a flat piece of wood, then painted on black squares with printer's ink. To make checkers he sliced a stick into round pieces the size of buttons, then painted half of them black. Now he and Joe play every evening by the fire.

July 3
Still at Fort Sanders

Mother and I are sharing things with Mrs. Rowe, particularly a large pot to put over our campfire so we can do laundry together. While I was stirring suds, Mrs. Rowe leaned over a washboard to scrub one of Ellie's dresses — her sleeves were rolled up and her hands were red from hot water.

She said that when they were in Nebraska Territory she saw girls and their mothers working on the railroad, swinging tools and digging. They were Indians from the Omaha tribe and earned 50 cents a day. Most of them were stronger than men. And they didn't wear bonnets to shade their faces. I would never work for the railroad, especially if doing so made my face get sunburned.

During the day I hide this journal inside my pillowcase so no one will find it to read. At night I put it under my blanket, down by my feet. When I turn over in sleep, I can feel it close to me.

Later

Joe found a friend his age named Richard and they've been playing together every day. This morning after breakfast they found a puppy. Maybe they were teasing it, I don't know, but when the puppy ran off they chased it right into the cows.

Well, before anyone could do anything there was a stampede. A bull broke away from the herd, galloped down the tracks, and charged a steam engine coming straight for him. He was struck dead. The cowcatcher, which looks like the engine's buck teeth, scooped the bull out of the way instead of squashing him. Some men were furious about this, because the stampede could have killed lots of people.

Richard got spanked by his uncle. Father took Joe for a long walk. Whether he got whipped or not I don't know, but today he's behaving himself. During breakfast Mother said, "Sterling, how are we ever going to keep Joe busy? We can't watch him every single moment." Later, I overheard her talking to Mrs. Rowe. Mother hadn't realized how hard it would be to keep Joe out of danger.

4th of July, 1868

A grand celebration today! A telegram arrived from Mr. Rowe wishing his family a happy day.

Mother and Mrs. Rowe (with Joe between them), along with several other ladies, roasted chickens all morning, but the stink of singed feathers . . . I preferred the sweet baking pies, dozens and dozens of them, made from peaches that had been brought in by train. Long tables were set up under shade trees near the creek that runs by the fort.

While the soldiers were busy eating, Ellie and I hiked around the bend to wade in the cool shallows, first taking off our heavy petticoats. When we were sure no one could see us, Ellie began a magnificent swoon. Up flew her arm, then with a graceful tilt she sank into the water. For a moment she let the current carry her lifeless body, then she popped to the surface, dripping and breathless.

"Oh," she cried, "Libby, you *must* try that, it's positively divine." And I did. We took turns so we could watch each other, but I'm sure her swoon was far better than mine. Later we lay on a grassy bank. The sun was so hot we soon were dry.

As sundown neared, the soldiers lit firecrackers. They still wear army pants from the war, gray with a dark stripe are the Johnny Rebs, blue pants with a dark stripe are the Yankees — Father and Pete wear theirs, too. The war is over but for the first time, Father says, we're all on the same side, trying to give our country a railroad that'll run coast to coast.

When the fireworks were over and folks lit lanterns to find their way back to camp, the soldiers — Blue and Gray — started singing together. First, "The Star-Spangled Banner," then "Amazing Grace."

Both Mother and Mrs. Rowe cried — I could see their wet cheeks in the lamplight.

July 12 or so

Now it is Pete who has a bad cold. He's been lying on his cot all day coughing, sneezing, and moaning. Every time he stands up his nose drips onto whatever is in front of him and his sleeves are wet from always wiping.

So Mother has offered to set the type. Her fingers are much smaller than Pete's, so she is fast, very fast.

First she reads what Father has written in his

notebook. She forms the sentence in her mind, then picks the metal letters out of their little boxes. I don't know how she does this because since the letters are backwards she must compose each word backwards. She arranges them in a small tray and starting at the top she spells things out from *right* to *left*. Large letters are for headlines, smaller ones for the story. When she's finished, the entire story is backwards, so if a looking glass was held up to it I could read it perfectly.

Last night when Mother blew out the lantern before bed, she whispered a secret to me: When Father was in the war she took a job at night, after Joe and I would go to sleep. Mrs. Cotton came to watch over us while Mother rode our horse Tipsy to the *Rocky Mountain News*. The editor was one of our neighbors, and whenever his compositor drank too much whiskey, he sent someone to our house to tell Mother he needed her help. She would check spelling and sometimes rewrite stories if they didn't make sense, and she also set type — now I know why the tips of her fingers were always stained black, from picking up the inky letters.

Another secret: I think Mother knows as much about writing and putting out a newspaper as Father does.

Joe got a whipping today and now I'm sorry that I wished for him to get in more trouble than I do.

Engine *No. 43* blew its whistle before starting to chug away from the station. I saw the engineer lean out his window and wave his cap to some boys who were playing on the cowcatcher, yelling for them to get off. When I saw that one of the boys was my own brother, I screamed.

I couldn't think of what words to call out to Father and Mother, so I just pointed. Father threw his ink roller to the ground, then ran and caught up to the engine, which was moving slowly. He grabbed Joe by the back of his shirt and dragged him off.

Mother and Father are worried now. I heard them whispering at night when they thought I was asleep. Father thinks he should send us back to Denver and go on without us, just him, Pete, and the printing press.

"Or," Father said, "we could try something else."

"What?" Mother asked.

"Julia," he said, "it'll be dangerous being on the front line, but maybe if we catch up to the crews and let Joe be a water boy he'll be too busy and too tired to get into trouble."

I strained to hear in the darkness. Mother sighed, then she whispered so softly it sounded like a breath.

"All right," she said.

Sunday, July 26

Several generals — Grant, Sherman, Sheridan, and Harney — had a big meeting today, with some of the Union Pacific bosses. Mr. Russell wanted to take their photographs, so they all stood outside in front of the dining hall and tried not to move. Ellie and I watched from the shade of a nice little pine tree, for it was terribly hot.

No one smiled! Among the men stood some ladies in white summer dresses, a few girls about my age, and a spotted dog that would not stop wagging its tail, it was so happy to be in the middle of everyone.

One of the girls brought her birdcage outside and hung it on a post just above General Ulysses S. Grant's head — he wore a white straw hat, and he chewed on a stogie the whole time we watched. When it was time for his picture, he took the cigar out of his mouth and set it in the dirt at his feet, then put his hands on the fence.

Joe said he hopes General Grant gets to be

president because he has the same initials as our
country: U.S.

Next day

We're heading west again. Mother and Father haven't
yet told Joe he gets to be a water boy, but meanwhile I
wonder, What can *I* do that will be important?

Father and Pete packed the press and equipment
back into the crates, then tied our trunks on top of everything. They rolled up the tents and strapped them on
back. I'm happy that Mrs. Rowe and Ellie are traveling
with us. They have a buckboard and two shiny black
horses to pull it. (Ellie and I traded bonnets for the day
so we could really truly feel like sisters.)

Mother is quiet. I can tell she's upset about something, but when I asked, she just fussed with a strand of
her hair that had fallen into her eyes, tucking it into her
net.

"Is it about Joe?" I asked.

"No."

"Mother, am I in trouble?"

"No, Libby, we'll talk later."

We're somewhere in the middle of Wyoming. The desert is scorching hot and the wind doesn't cool us off. The backs of my hands are reddish-brown from sunburn. My bonnet shades my face, but it sticks out so far along my cheeks that it is like blinders on a horse — I can only see things right in front of me. Sometimes I just want to rip it off my head and stomp on it.

Mother and I sewed stones into our hems to keep our skirts from blowing up and over our heads. We saw that happen to one lady in front of a saloon, but she didn't seem to care that the whole world saw her bloomers (bright green satin!). This saloon was near the tracks — in a small town made entirely of tents, no log or stone buildings. Mother and Father said that Joe and I are never to go near this town.

"Why?" I asked.

"Don't argue, Libby."

Mother said we'd talk, but now she says not to argue. I'm so upset they won't tell me what this is all about, I just sit in the shade by our tent. Ellie's mother also said, "Stay away," but not why. After supper we took a walk and whispered a plan. Tonight when everyone's asleep, she and I will see that little town for ourselves. We don't care what our parents say.

July 29

About last night. I'm so glad to have this diary because I need to tell what happened but am too ashamed to speak of it to anyone.

I waited until Mother and Father slept. I pulled my dress down over my nightshirt (for I had hidden it earlier under my blanket) and felt in the darkness for my shoes, which were under my cot. Quietly I crept outside to Ellie's tent and scratched on the canvas. In a moment she and I were hurrying to the edge of camp. My hair was loose so the breeze lifted it behind my shoulders — I felt wonderfully free.

It was dark except for the blaze of lights coming from the little town. Torchlight showed that the canvas tents were all sizes, some square, some pointed like tipis. I recognized piano music and banjos, dancing and loud singing. Suddenly shouting came from across the street, followed by several gunshots. Was someone murdered? I worried, glad that Ellie and I were hiding in the shadows. We looped arms together for safety.

"Let's go closer," she said into my ear. So we did, finding a dark alley between buildings. From here we could see that Main Street was just a muddy path. I wondered about the mud because there'd been no rain for days, but soon I smelled why. Every foul odor that comes from kitchens and chamber pots and horses must have been dumped into the street. It was dreadful.

From our alley we saw three ladies leaning against a hitching rail, all fancied up. They were watching men walk in and out of the saloons and couldn't see us.

When someone grabbed my arm, I cried out in surprise, so did Ellie.

"Wanna dance?" said a man's voice. It was too dark to see his face, but I smelled his breath. Whiskey or some such. He was a small man, about my height, so I was stunned by his strength when he forced me, with Ellie clinging to my other arm, to the front of a saloon. We were standing in a puddle and I could feel cold mud seep into my shoes. The three ladies looked at us. Were they smiling or was it their lip rouge that made it appear so?

The man was clean shaven, wearing a white shirt, a string tie, and a black satin vest. "You're gonna dance with me, little girlies," he said, pulling us both through the swinging doors.

I turned around, trying to break free, but his grip tightened. "Ellie, run," I said, but her eyes were wide with terror. She was too frightened to move.

The saloon was loud with shouting and music, cigar smoke was so heavy my eyes stung. A bearded man captured Ellie around the waist and began dancing with her through the crowd. I saw her hair swing over her shoulder, then she was a blur because the man with the string tie was whirling me around and around in a dance. Men watching us burst into cheers.

I struggled to free myself, but felt dizzy and sick. I wanted to scream for help, but did not want Mother and Father to see me like this, a foolish, sorry girl. *Why hadn't I listened to them?*

When I saw that Ellie was being dragged to a doorway at the back of the saloon, I twisted my arm free and tried to follow her.

"Oh, no you don't, little lady," the man said to me, grabbing my hair. I don't know where I found the strength, but I jabbed my elbow into his stomach and with my other hand slapped him hard across the face. He let go.

"Ellie!" I called through the noise. When I reached her she was beating her fists against the man's chest, her face red with anger. I pulled his beard as hard as I could and kicked him. Maybe he was drunk or maybe he changed his mind, but he dropped Ellie to the floor.

We pushed our way through the cheering men, out into the night, running, running. Halfway back to camp I looked behind us and when I saw no one was following, my knees buckled. Ellie and I clung to each other on the cold ground, sobbing with relief.

I can't put into words my embarrassment, my shame. Ellie and I could hardly speak we were so out of breath. In the darkness we touched each other's faces and hair to make sure the other was all right. I felt cold air on my shoulder where my sleeve had torn. Buttons were missing from her collar. When a man carrying a lantern approached us, we quickly backed away into the shadows, but his light found us.

"Libby!" called Father. "Ellie!" First he asked if we were all right. He held his lantern high, and when he saw my torn dress he caught his breath. "Oh, Daughter."

More later. Mother's calling. . . .

To continue about last night . . .

Father lectured us right there at the edge of camp with the black, moonless sky over us like an umbrella. The air was dark and heavy as if it was about to rain.

He told us that he had woken suddenly and, not seeing me in bed, started for Ellie's tent, but heard our frightened voices in the distance. He ran until he found us.

He called that little town "Hell on Wheels." It's a temporary town — people put up stores, cafes, and saloons for a week or more, then when tracks have been laid further on, down come the tents. Some 60 miles further, up go the tents again, like a traveling circus.

"Girls," he said, "as you may now guess, everything immoral and cruel that can happen, does. There are drifters, outlaws, fast dollar types, and worse." He said if he ever caught me sneaking out again, he would whip me, then we would return to Denver immediately.

At this Ellie and I both started to cry again. "I'm so sorry, Mr. West," she said. "It was my fault."

"No," I said, "it was mine. Father, please forgive me."

Another day

Ellie and I alone carry our secret, for Father did not tell our mothers and he's not spoken further of it. Sometimes we whisper about what could have happened if we hadn't escaped, but then we stop ourselves. How can we know what we don't know? We've agreed to stay far, far away from that little terrible, horrible town.

The days are still very hot. At this moment I'm tired of looking at desert. Every time a wagon drives by there are clouds of dust. My bonnet keeps the top of my head clean, but my braids are powdery from the blowing sand. It seems my shoes are always dirty, my fingernails, too, and the front of my dress has tiny holes from sparks. Campfires singe anything that gets too close, and you have to get close to cook.

I'm afraid I'm very far from looking like a lady, even though I quickly mended my sleeve. If Mrs. Cotton or Kate and Annie saw me now, they'd think I look like an emigrant.

Pete's cold has worsened into bronchitis. He works with Father for a few hours each day, but then he must rest because he can't stop coughing. It is most unpleasant to be around him so I stay away.

August 1

Having stones sewed into my hem makes my dress heavier. I wish I could wear cotton trousers like Joe. He doesn't have to worry about a strong gust of wind showing everyone his underclothes. He can climb onto a wagon, then jump down without embarrassment. Whatever troubles Joe has from being a boy, I envy his freedom.

This prompted Ellie and me to do something shocking. In her tent she opened her trunk. Folded neatly in the bottom are her father's extra clothes, including two pairs of waist coveralls. With dramatic flair Ellie stepped out of her skirt and flung it over her cot, then stepped into the trousers. They were big and baggy, but I helped her thread a scarf around the waist to cinch them up (we couldn't find suspenders). She marched with high knees in a little circle, laughing.

"Libby, you do it!"

Soon I, too, was dressed like a man, marching in a

circle until I was dizzy. Thus, we enjoyed our morning until Mother called our names, for it was time for schoolwork. We packed away the clothes and emerged from the tent, ladies once again. If it were considered proper, Ellie and I would like to wear pants every day.

Later

There was near panic this afternoon because telegraph lines were down. Folks said Indians did it, they were coming our way, and we'd all be killed.

Some men pumped a handcar several miles east while others on horseback (with shotguns) rode alongside, to see what was the matter. They found several lines knocked down and noticed the lower parts of the telegraph poles had dark brown hair sticking to them.

Human scalps, someone said. But a wiser man examined the hair and said, "Buffalo." It seems the animals use the poles as scratching posts, to rub off their thick winter coats. Buffalo are so strong they uproot the poles like little trees. Mostly they do this in the spring, but some are still roaming around in the summer needing a good scratch. (I wonder what buffalo did before the telegraph went up.)

When the men returned to camp, they steered the handcar onto a side track and left it. No one but myself was watching when Joe and another boy climbed up the iron wheels and sneaked onto the platform. They each grabbed a handle and tried to pump up and down, as if they were on a seesaw. The cart didn't move. For ten minutes they bent over and stood up, over and up, but if they rolled forward it was only a few inches.

"Hey, you kids!" someone yelled, then cursed. "Get outa here!"

I'll not tell Mother about this. Luckily, Joe doesn't have the strength of four men or he and that handcar might have ended up who-knows-where.

August 2
Still in Wyoming somewhere

My dark thoughts toward Pete bother me. I think I must do a kindness for him, so that I myself will *feel* kind.

As he still has a heavy cough, he moved his bedroll to the back of our wagon. From the kettle over our campfire I poured some boiling water into a bowl, then added some cold until the water felt comfortable. I rolled up a cloth with a small piece of soap and carried it to him. He was lying against his satchel, his eyes closed. I set the water down by his legs and jiggled his foot.

"Pete, I thought this might make you feel better."

He opened his eyes and leaned forward, dipping his fingers in the warm water.

"Oh, Miss Libby, this is nice. Thank you."

I backed away, feeling guilty. (Am I selfish for wishing he would bathe?)

All afternoon I've been helping Mother salt a side of beef and pack it in bags. The blood makes my hands sticky and the salt stings every little crack along my fingertips — this is not my favorite chore. So when Mother sent me to bring a pail of hot water for washing, I was happy to do so. Remembering the bowl I'd left with Pete, I returned to the wagon.

He was sitting up and had a smile, his face as clean and bare as a boy's — he had shaved his whiskers! His hair was wet, combed back from his forehead, and under his vest was a clean shirt, blue flannel with the sleeves rolled up to his elbows. He was holding his pocket watch, which he clicked shut when he noticed me.

"Four-fifteen sharp," he said to himself, then, "Hello, Miss Libby."

After a moment of staring at him I said, "Pete, how old are you?"

"Near my nineteenth birthday."

"No you're not."

"Indeed, I am."

"Well, when did you join the army?" I asked, still thinking he was trying to fool me.

"Twelve," he answered. "As a drummer boy for the Yanks."

I couldn't think of anything to say. I had thought Pete was much older, maybe closer to Father's age, like an uncle. Something else surprised me — for the first time I had noticed the color of his eyes.

Cerulean blue. I'm glad I learned how to spell that.

Later

Something keeps going through my mind and I don't know what to make of it. Pete is only four years older than I am.

Knowing Pete is closer to my age than Father's makes me feel more like myself — it's like talking to my own brother instead of a man I have to treat with respect.

Pete was sitting by the campfire after supper with a tin cup of coffee. He looked up when I sat across from him.

"Evenin', Miss Libby."

"Hello." I pulled one of my clean handkerchiefs from my apron pocket. Just that morning I pressed it. (The iron was so hot from the coals I burned my thumb.) I leaned around the fire and touched his elbow with it.

"Here," I said. "So you won't have to use your sleeve."

He spread the cloth over his knee and when he saw the corner where my initials were embroidered, he ran his finger over the blue threads.

"Pretty," he said.

"It's for you, Pete, so you can stop being a barbarian. Everyone knows gentlemen use a handkerchief."

"Is that so?" Laughing, he shook his head. He set his cup in the dirt and picked up a stick to poke the fire. "Miss Libby, you are the bossiest girl I ever did know."

I stood up and turned on my heel to find Ellie. She doesn't think I'm bossy.

August 4

Today's news from the telegraph is that President Johnson recently signed an act of Congress that makes Wyoming an official territory of the United States. The boundaries now include parts of Dakota, Idaho, and Utah. Father said that because of the railroad, the towns of Cheyenne and Laramie will soon be important enough to have their own local governments.

Another telegram from Mr. Rowe. He met some friendly Indians and traded his hat for a beaded neck-lace for Ellie.

August 5

Today more news came over the wire from Washington City. The telegraph operator had a mad face when he read the report.

"The Fourteenth Amendment to the U.S. Constitution is official," he said. "Like it or not, folks, Negroes born in this country are citizens, same with Chi-nee born here."

But Father said, "Hooray, it's about time." Mother said, "Amen."

They explained that anyone who's born in America, no matter the color of his skin or the country his parents came from, is a citizen. "With all the rights and protections our Constitution has to offer," Father said.

"Indians, too?" I asked

Father removed his hat and combed his fingers through his hair. "Well," he said, "everyone except Indians."

"But why?"

He took a notebook from inside his jacket, then put on his eyeglasses, hooking the wires over each ear. "Let me show you something, Libby." He read something General William Tecumseh Sherman said last year, after Indians had ambushed and killed Captain Fetterman, nearly 80 soldiers, and a few civilians. These are the general's words:

We must act with vindictive earnestness against the Sioux, even to their extermination, men, women, and children.

I didn't know what to say. Did General Sherman really mean that Indian *children* and their *mothers* should be killed? How can he think this way? Father said he was named after Tecumseh, chief of the Shawnee, one of the most respected Indians in America. I think he dishonors his parents who named him and he dishonors a good man (even though I never saw Tecumseh with my own eyes).

When I noticed General Sherman that day in the Laramie Hotel I knew he wasn't a gentleman, the way he let his soup spill onto the tablecloth, and now this. Mother, Father, and Joe are in our tent, ready for bed, but before we blow out the lantern, two thoughts:

1. General Sherman may be the tallest man in the army, but in my opinion he is small.
2. I guess the color of your skin does matter.

August 7

Now that Pete isn't coughing so much he brought his bedroll back into our tent. But I'm uneasy about this. I don't want him to see me in my nightgown.

When Mother saw me hiding under my blanket to get

undressed, she understood what I hadn't been able to express. She took Pete's things out to the wagon. Through our thin canvas wall I could hear her speaking gently to him.

"Pete," she said, "it's best you sleep out here now."

"Of course, Mrs. West."

I'm not mad at Mother anymore for bringing me here. I love it that she knows me. I watched Pete play checkers with Joe and thought to myself, *What a kind fellow*.

August 10

We caught up to the Union Pacific work train, and what a sight, it is like a rolling factory. Father said it's called Casement's Army because the foreman, Jack Casement, is as hardworking and organized as a general. In the coming days I will try to describe it more so when I'm old and want to remember, I will be able to read these pages.

Meanwhile Mrs. Rowe and Ellie are camped next to us and Pete, too. We are on the opposite side of the tracks from all the saloons and such — Father has seen to that. Ellie and I have no desire to explore these places anyway.

There are other families nearby, respectable ones. A man gave Father a roll of canvas so he and Pete were able to sew new walls to their newspaper office, to replace the ones that had burned. Now the printing press will be out of the rain, if it should storm.

Two fellows came to visit with handshakes and loud hellos. It was the Freeman brothers. Father doesn't say their Christian names, he just calls them "boys." "Howdy, boys," like that. Even though they and Father fought on opposite sides in the war and are now competing with one another for business, they are friendly to each other. To hear them talk, I think it's because of the railroad. They're excited about such a grand thing being done for America, and they're excited to be reporting about it. They even showed us a telegram that said Union Pacific is winning the Great Race by a long stretch.

The Freemans invited us to their campsite to see their Washington Hand Press. It's similar to ours, but much larger and heavier. Their office is a wider tent than Father's, for they bunk there and cook, as well. A square, iron stove has a smokestack pointing out of a hole in the canvas.

Oh, but it was messy. Stacks of paper were every-where. Their clothes were thrown on their beds and were hanging here and there. It looked like they'd just done some washing or needed to.

And there were mice droppings on their table! Maybe our tents are cleaner because Mother knows about these things. She will not tolerate prairie dogs or other rodents.

Later

At supper Joe announced that he wants to be a head spiker.

"What's that, darling?" asked Mother.

When Joe described the men who hammer spikes down into the rails, her smile faded.

"That's just what we need," she said. "A seven-year-old boy with a hammer and no supervision."

August 11

Instead of a caboose at the back of the train, there are two steam engines that *push* the cars along. In front of the engines is a boxcar with a kitchen and pantry. When Ellie, Joe, and I peaked inside we saw several sides of beef hanging from hooks. It looked like they were covered with peppercorns, but when the cook hit his long wooden spoon against the beef, the pepper lifted off for a moment before returning to the meat. They were flies!

The car in front of this one is for dining. There is one long table running through its middle with benches on each side. Nailed onto each table, a few inches apart, are tin plates for men to eat off. Nailed down!

The cook is an old Irishman with a thick, white mustache. He wears an apron that comes down to the tops of his boots and for some reason everyone calls him "Miss Sallie." When he leaned out the door to dump a bucket of slops, we asked about the plates.

"Miss Sallie, how do you wash them?"

"We don't," he said. "Too much time and trouble."

When he saw that we were speechless he said, "Listen here, girlies. Soon as a man finishes, there's a fellow behind him needing to eat, and a fellow behind him. See what I mean? When everyone's done, why then we swab 'em."

We went back to the dining car and counted the plates, more than a hundred, so we figured that at each meal probably four men used the same plate. Ellie and I are going to write our friends back home. Kate and Annie won't believe it.

For supper we had stew. As I ladled the steaming broth into our bowls, I asked why the cook is called Miss Sallie.

Pete swallowed his mouthful of cornbread, then lifted his napkin to his lips. "When fellas are lonesome," he said, "they like to give their cooks a nickname. It makes 'em feel more to home."

But Joe said, "I think it's a stupid name for a man."

August 24

About the work train: In front of the dining car are three boxcars as tall as barns, each one has three levels of bunk beds inside. Ellie and I peeked in one, but it stunk so bad we decided we needed to look no further. Men have pitched tents outside up on the roofs, also in the dirt alongside the tracks. Some hang hammocks under the belly of the train. Father said sleeping quarters are less cramped this way, as there are more than 400 workers in Casement's Army.

Later, when Ellie and I were alone in her tent, relaxing in her father's trousers, we laughed about the real reason men camp outside. It's because of their own stink!

Speaking of things that smell bad, privies are temporary holes dug beyond the tracks. There is no privacy, so Ellie and I keep our eyes to ourselves. We ladies and Mrs. Rowe use the night jars in our tent, then take them out to pour them under sagebrush and cover with sand.

After our morning lessons Ellie and I like to watch the men work. They have such a smooth, swift rhythm we feel as though we're seeing a ballet of strong men. Some of them sing about working on the railroad, some whistle old battle songs, and some are stone silent, with sweat running down their faces.

If the tracks need to veer left or right, men called rail benders pound their sledgehammers against the iron until curves are formed. The most amazing thing is how quickly this all goes. A section of track is finished faster than it takes me to write about it. Father says that on a good day they can finish between two and four miles, sometimes more.

He also said most of the workers are from Ireland, but I have also seen many freed slaves. There are war veterans, too, both Yanks and Rebs. Mother and I watched Joe carry a bucket of water to a group of them. We could tell which army they'd been in by the color of their pants. They took turns drinking, some from the same cup.

"Thank goodness," Mother said. "We're all on the same side now."

August 25

This brings me to Joe's job. As it is August, the days are hot. Some afternoons it will cloud up for a quick thundershower, but the rain lasts just a few minutes. It cools the air briefly and leaves behind a wonderful aroma of sagebrush. But rain or not, the workers need water every hour.

Joe first turns a spigot on one of the water barrels and fills his bucket. He wears a rope around his waist with several tin cups dangling from it, hooked on by their handles. The clanging makes him sound like a farmer's goat, but I've not told him so. He's very proud of his important job.

"Doesn't he sound manly?" Mother asked Father, loud enough for Joe to hear.

"Why, yes, he does," Father answered. "Just like the workers who wear tool belts."

But last night I heard them whispering in the tent. The

real reason they like Joe's clanging cups is because they can hear where he is. Mother said that as far as jobs go she's just glad he's not a cabin boy far out to sea, like Father was when he was young.

Later

Have been feeling guilty about something. Back a few weeks ago, when Pete took off his shirt to swim in the creek, I spent more time looking at him than I should have. His chest and arms are muscular and for one brief moment I wanted him to put those strong arms around me. (Am I wrong for thinking this?)

To me he looks as strong as the railroad men. Yesterday after the noon meal Ellie and I busied ourselves near a supply wagon so we could again watch the workers.

The iron men had just dropped two rails in place, side by side, a few feet apart. Then came the mule whackers who lowered the heavy wooden ties across the rails, making it look like a long ladder lying on the ground. Immediately a man followed with a tool that resembled a large letter *T* and placed it over the ties to make sure the spaces were even.

Ellie said her father once explained that these measurements must be absolutely, one hundred percent perfect otherwise speeding trains might fall off the track! Oh, I hope this *T*-man is careful.

August 27

Every day after breakfast Ellie and I clean up the dishes and brush crumbs off the table. We bring out our slates to practice penmanship, arithmetic, and to help Joe with his letters. He is still working hard to finish *Two Years Before the Mast*, though he's only on page 93 (there are 338, not counting the glossary on sailing terms).

Mother reads from newspaper articles to explain government and world politics. For instance, the big mess in the White House. Our seventeenth president, Andrew Johnson, has lots of enemies in Congress who tried to impeach him. I didn't know presidents could be fired. He took over when Abe Lincoln was assassinated and for some reason he's unpopular.

Mother folded the newspapers and tucked them into a box with our slates, then opened the dictionary. She looked up "impeach," then had us spell it out loud and define it.

"Abraham Lincoln was a wonderful president," she said. "It would be hard for any man to fill his shoes."

September 1

We've moved camp again to follow the railroad, and are now at Fort Bridger, still in the territory of Wyoming. Some Mormons work at this trading post and have been very friendly to us. One of them said Central Pacific is now in the lead by a hundred miles, but then his friend corrected him, saying that *we* are ahead. Once again, I don't know who to believe!

The packing and unpacking of the printing press and all the equipment is wearing Father out. His legs ache and I see him rubbing them every morning, for that was where he was wounded. (He has never let me see the scar.)

We are getting closer to the border of Utah Territory. The land looks dry. The days are still hot, yet at night the air is crisp and cold — autumn is coming! My favorite time of day now is evening, after supper, when we're around the campfire. Wood is scarce so we use anything we can gather, old stumps of sagebrush, horse dung, even cow patties, though it's hard to start wet ones.

There is some wood for sale in the trading post, but most of it is needed to build trestles and bridges. It's expensive, too, being hauled in from the Black Hills area.

Later

This morning after our lessons, Ellie and I walked about a half-mile away from camp and then westward along the newly laid tracks. We could hear the ping and clang of hammers hitting spikes, over and over, the rhythm that has become music to all of us. Every blow of iron against iron means we're getting closer to finishing the Great Race.

While we watched men carry the rails and ties to lay in the roadbed, I confided in Ellie. Things about Pete. Such as, I find him interesting, but I don't know how to talk to him without being bossy. Also, I like to look at his face, for his eyes are kind.

"I know," she said.

"You do?"

"Libby, every time he looks at you, your cheeks turn bright red."

Now I wonder. Does Mother see me blush, or Father? Does Pete notice? I wish I knew what he thinks of me!

September 2

A curious thing. I've noticed that every time we take down our tent to move camp, we must knock down a wasp nest. When we put the tent back up a day or so later, a new family of wasps is waiting for us and they immediately get busy making a home. The only way to keep them out is to build a smoky fire inside, but that could burn things down.

"It's just something we'll have to live with," Mother says.

Now I'm sitting on my cot. The canvas wall behind me glows with afternoon sunlight. And overhead are five gold-and-black wasps walking slowly around and around their new nest. It is the size of an almond.

Joe wants to poke at it with a stick, but I won't let him. This may sound odd, but the wasps remind me of Mother. Wherever we are she hurries up to make a cozy, safe place for us.

Our beds are the first thing she readies, folding our warm quilts at the end, our pillows plumped up on top of the sheet. Joe and I each have a small trunk with clothes and whatnots, which she puts by our cots to use as a sitting place during the day.

Lately Mrs. Rowe and Mother have not boiled water for laundry, but instead have just washed the dust out of things. They stretched a rope between our tents for our shirts and stockings to dry in the sun. Every other day Mother hangs out our blankets and pillowcases, so at night when Joe and I go to sleep we have the fragrance of sunshine and fresh air at our cheeks.

As the days get cooler and the sun goes down earlier, we are quicker to bed. I worry about Father — he limps badly in the mornings and with each passing day he moves more slowly. I know Mother worries about him, but she doesn't say a word.

Later

I heard Father tell Mother that he is earning enough money from his newspaper ads to pay for the groceries we buy in "town." But several store owners have not paid Father for the advertisements he printed, and he wonders if they ever will.

"We need more newsprint," he told Mother. "And we just opened our last bucket of ink." To order these things from Omaha he must pay in advance and wait days, maybe weeks, until they're delivered this far west.

It makes me nervous to hear them worry about money.

Something else that makes me anxious, but not in a bad way, is this Great Race. Are we winning or losing? We don't know. It's hard to believe there are other railroad workers moving fast and furious toward us when we can't see them or hear them. It's grand to think we may soon be face-to-face!

September 3

Last night during campfire Pete touched my arm and leaned close to me. "Do you want to take a walk, Miss Libby?" he asked.

Did I! I was thrilled he wanted to be with me, but while I buttoned my cloak I felt nervous. What would we talk about? What if I said something stupid?

Moonlight made the rails look silvery and in the distance we could see the Wasatch Mountains of Utah. Our breath was frost in the cold air and I was sorry I'd not worn my wool leggings — it seems just days ago that I packed them away in my trunk. We walked beyond camp along the tracks until the rails ended in soft dirt. The narrow roadbed continued far into the desert, prepared weeks earlier by surveyors and graders who are now miles west.

After five minutes of watching the starry sky, I was beginning to shiver with cold. I tried not to stare at Pete, but his face is so nice to look at. His jaw is strong and the way his hair curls at his neck, well, I think he's handsome. I rubbed my arms for warmth, wishing I could think of something interesting to say. Pete glanced at me as if he himself wanted to speak, but instead he reached in his vest pocket and pulled out his watch. Clicking it open, he held it toward the moonlight.

"Well," he said, "it's almost nine-thirty, guess we should be getting back."

"All right."

That's all we said to each other the whole evening! I'm so upset with myself for being mute. He must think I've nothing in my head.

September 6

Father printed a story in his paper today that has most of us worried. Somewhere east of us, Indians (he doesn't know from which tribe) managed to pry apart some rails, which caused a speeding train to crash. In the locomotive, the man who keeps the fire going was thrown against the firebox and burned to death. Passengers scared away the Indians by shooting rifles they'd kept in racks above the seats. Mother is horrified by this account. While I cleared the dishes after supper, Pete and Father talked about why the Indians are mad. They don't want the railroad because it's ruining their hunting grounds and chasing off the buffalo. Also, the army's campaigns against them have caused too many innocent families to be killed.

Hearing this makes me feel sad for the Indians, not afraid.

September 21

Mother has given me a job to do, one that she says is extremely important. I'm to check the spelling in Father's newspaper!

This afternoon in our printing office she called out, "Libby, look this up." She pronounced a word I didn't understand, but I guessed the first three letters and went from there. I opened our big dictionary. It's quite heavy and must be set on a table. The pages are full of inky fingerprints: Father's, Pete's, Mother's, and now mine. Found the word.

It was *expeditious*, which means speedy or prompt. Father's sentence was *Union Pacific is trying to be expeditious*, but he misspelled it. I peered down onto the page layout, took a pair of tweezers, and pulled out some of the middle letters. Careful not to drop these tiny metal pieces, I walked to the shelf and returned each letter to its proper box. I picked out others to make the correction, then with my tweezers carefully set the backwards letters in place. I like my new job, but it's hard to look up words if you don't know how they're spelled.

Joe is being a good brother. He is so exhausted at the end of the day from carrying pails of water everywhere, he just sits sleepily by the fire, no trouble. Before bed I read one page to him from his sailing book. By then I myself am falling asleep.

September 22

Sunny, cold days. No rain or snow, thankfully. The workers in Casement's Army inch forward day by day. It feels as if it's taking forever.

National news: In Connecticut a train crashed into Naugatuck River. Ten people drowned, including some children. I wonder if the tracks were safe, which makes me join in Mother's worries. What if Union Pacific is being careless about safety while they try to win the Great Race?

October 7
Still in Fort Bridger

Have been busy helping Mother and Pete publish the newspaper, as Father is ill. His legs ache so bad, he spends most of the day sitting in the back of the wagon, feeling ashamed and sorry he brought us all out in the middle of nowhere.

Mother tries to cheer him up. "It's all right," she says. "Our family is together."

I didn't know something about Father and it scared me when I found out today. He was shot twice in his legs, when he tried to escape from Andersonville prison. (I also hadn't known he tried to escape!) Fragments from the lead bullets are still buried in his flesh. It was hoped the pieces would eventually work their way out as often happens with wounds, but that isn't the case. Mother worries there's infection.

A quick note before bed.

When Pete and I stand next to each other at the printing press, I come up to his shoulder. He smells good, like campfire smoke and fresh air. Yesterday I tripped over the ink pail, falling against his arm, and for a moment he held me as I struggled to my feet. I'm sure I blushed, but secretly it felt wonderful. Did he notice?

Anyway, when I'm keeping my mind on the newspaper we work well together. He's gentle about correcting my mistakes, for twice I've set headlines upside down. He's also good humored because now and then *I* correct his spelling.

"All right, boss," he says as he resets the type.

I believe I'm growing fond of Pete. It seems odd, but now when we're together I feel happy and when we're not together I find myself thinking about him, hoping he'll walk by.

Oh, another bit of news before the candle goes . . . there's one more tunnel to cut through the Wasatch Mountains, then tracks can be laid. This means we'll finally be able to look out over the Great Salt Lake Valley and maybe see workers from California! At last Crocker's Pets will meet Casement's Army. I can't believe it.

October 11

Woke in the middle of the night to Father screaming. I was terrified, for I'd never heard him cry out so. Mother lit a candle and said, "What's wrong, what's wrong?" In the light her braid looked silky, and she quickly pulled a shawl around her for warmth. There was frost in the air from her breathing hard.

"Sterling!" she cried, rubbing his arms, trying to comfort him. Father was having a nightmare and his legs ached so bad he couldn't move.

This morning at breakfast Mother spoke to us. "We must hurry to Salt Lake City," she said. "Pete, I need your help so we can leave tomorrow."

Pete was spooning sugar into his hot tea. He wore a brown leather coat over his shirt, for the air was cold, even in front of the fire.

"Miss Julia," he said, "I'll do anything for you folks."

We're camped at Muddy Creek. The printing press is in the wagon, covered with a tarp. Mother drives, sometimes letting Joe take the reins. Father sits next to him on the bench, a wool blanket wrapped snugly over his legs. He is silent in pain. In the morning after breakfast Mother heats our two irons in the coals, then sets them under Father's feet and Joe's. I wonder how she keeps her own feet warm.

As there's no room in the wagon for me, I walk. So does Pete. When I get too cold I swing my arms and stomp my feet and if I look like a soldier I don't care. It's getting easier for us to talk to each other. Pete told me that during the war Father read to him, letters from home, newspaper articles. Father even gave him a book of psalms he found on a battlefield. Now Pete's favorite thing besides being a journalist is to read.

A few days ago we camped about 20 miles from Fort Bridger. Mother drove the mules to the outskirts of a noisy town, and on the way passed a tent with *Frontier Index* painted on its side. Father called "Hello!" and out came the Freeman brothers, their hands covered in ink.

"Wait till you see our next editorial," one of the

brothers told us. "It's time to clean up these lawless railroad towns, close the saloons and gambling halls, or ban liquor, something."

The next morning we pulled out early, while it was dark. The Freemans were still sleeping as we saw no smoke coming from their little chimney.

October 19

Yesterday we passed through Echo Canyon, over the backbone of the Wasatch Mountains. The walls were high and rugged so sunlight hit only the upper ridges. In crevices of rock I could see ice and patches of snow. We hurried as fast as our mules would pull for the trail was in deep, cold shade.

We're now camped in a quiet little Mormon town called Echo City, some miles west of Ogden. At the base of one of the cliffs, there's a stone house that was a Pony Express station where my cousin Jimmy, who was a rider, once stayed (his father is my uncle Henry).

Ellie and I walked past the stone station and turned into a meadow where we found a creek. We threw rocks to break the ice crusting along the bank. While we were bending down to drink the cold, sweet water, a girl about five years old came up to us. She held out two red apples.

We thanked her and asked where she lived. She pointed to a cabin on the far side of the creek, where several children were playing out front. Nearby a woman sat in the sunshine working a spinning wheel, another lady was churning butter, another was sweeping the porch.

I was remembering that Mormon men have many wives, but I was having trouble knowing what to ask the girl. I was so curious my eyes were popping, but I wanted to be kind. "Your mother?" was all I said.

"Oh," she answered, "they's my aunties. Ma's in bed nursing the new baby."

Ellie and I wanted to know more *details*, but the girl turned away and skipped down the path that ran along the creek. Our chance to learn about Mormons firsthand was gone, at least for now.

Later

A sudden storm came up this afternoon. It was so windy, Mother and I dug a narrow trench three feet long and ten inches deep, then built our cooking fire at the bottom. When good flames caught the wood, we set the Dutch oven on top where it straddled the trench perfectly, the pot of water next to it.

After supper we laid potatoes among the coals, covered them with sand, and this morning ate them for breakfast with fried pork fat and cups of cocoa. The biscuits I baked turned out black on the bottom and raw on top.

Father is feeling better today. He says that from this point, the railroad heads northwest, but our family will travel southwest, along the old Mormon Trail, following Brigham Young's steps. Father says that even though we won't be with the railroad crews, he can still pick up telegraphed news, write about it, and print it.

And he can still wire stories down to the *Rocky Mountain News*. Maybe there'll be more shop owners willing to buy ads from him, willing to pay him on time.

"I'm not extending any more credit," Father told me. "I've been nice, I've been patient, but I can't feed my family on good feelings."

I don't understand why people break promises. Don't they know Father depends on their honesty so that he himself can make an honest living?

We're staying with Uncle Henry in his cozy house behind his shop, "Spoon's Fancy Store." There is so much to tell, but for now will report the latest big news: Mr. U.S. Grant has been elected U.S. President, our country's eighteenth.

My cousin Thomas (he's eleven years old) wants me to help with the cider press. More later.

Later

Father is much better, but he does limp. The other morning, Mother patted his knee and cried, "Ouch!" She looked at her finger and it was bleeding. Somehow during the night, a tiny piece of shrapnel had worked its way through Father's skin, just the smallest piece. We crowded round to look, and even in the lantern light all we could see was a gray dot, like a flea.

Mother asked Pete to get tweezers from our printing kit, and he did. She distracted Father by telling him about Joe's latest mischief, and while his head was back in laughter, she pressed the tweezers over his leg and yanked out the metal. He cried out more in surprise than pain (he said later). It looked as if someone had drawn a red line on his skin, about an inch long, that's all the blood there was.

He said Mother's operation hadn't hurt, but he did sleep all afternoon. I think it interesting that wounds from the War Between the States are still healing. And even though Mother wasn't on a battlefield or in a prison camp, a Confederate's gunshot did make her bleed.

About the railroad. Workers are almost done tunneling through the Wasatch Mountains. Now that I myself have crossed over and seen the rugged peaks, I can imagine the cold and hard work those men must be enduring. The Great Race is still on because of their courage, because they refuse to give up.

I'm thankful to be in a warm, snug house. And to see Mother so happy. My aunt Clara is busy making us feel to home. Thomas's nine older sisters are married, and so is his brother Jimmy (I wish *I* had nine sisters!). Thus my family has one bedroom all to ourselves: a bed for Mother and Father, a trundle for Joe, and a little couch for me. A Lady Franklin stove in the hallway keeps this part of the house warm.

Pete has put up a tent behind Uncle Henry's house, in the yard leading to the orchard. At night his tent glows with lantern light, for he's reading a book he bought in Uncle Henry's store, called *A Tale of Two Cities*, by Charles Dickens. I would like to ask him to take a walk with me, but worry he'll think I'm too forward. Or if he said no, I would feel crushed.

Something puzzles me. When Pete and I were on the trail walking, it was easy to talk to each other and we laughed as friends. So why now, when he smiles at me from across the room, am I at a loss for words?

Ellie and her mother are staying one block away at Hotel Utah. Mr. Rowe recently sent them a telegram and said Union Pacific is laying a railbed across the northern tip of the Great Salt Lake. Though his message was short, two words gave me a thrill: *Saw Chinese.*

November 6

I've not written much about my schoolwork because once it's finished I don't want to repeat it here. But when our lessons and chores are done Ellie and I like to walk around town.

Every day we pass Brigham Young's house, hoping to

meet some of his children. His estate is surrounded by a stone wall, nine feet tall, but the other day one of the gates was ajar so we peeked into the yard. There were stacks of firewood, some bare fruit trees, and nearby a kitchen window was open. We could hear ladies talking and we could smell the good aroma of roast potatoes and beef. It seemed they were preparing the noon meal.

A door slammed and out hurried a girl about ten years old, with a shawl over her shoulders and high-topped boots, the laces undone. She disappeared around a corner, then a minute later came back holding her apron in front of her like a bowl, filled with eggs we guessed.

"Hello, little girl," I called, but she didn't hear me. The door slammed again, then someone shut the kitchen window.

Snow was beginning to fall, large white flakes swirling in the air, swirling down onto our arms. Ellie's dark braids were spotted white. We'd been standing in the cold for 15 minutes and were beginning to shiver. Now the sidewalks were white, the sky was white, our breath was white puffs in front of us as we hurried down the street to Uncle Henry's.

There were no customers in the store, just a few men,

including Father and Pete, sitting around the stove. Snow from our shoes melted into puddles on the hardwood floor. Ellie and I found a mop to clean up, then we took turns with the feather duster, going along the shelves and ledges. Windows are as tall as the ceiling, so we must climb a ladder to clean them. From up high I could see around the store and hear everything that's said. I like to help my uncle, but I also enjoy hearing the men talk.

"Libby," said Ellie, "you're eavesdropping."

"I know," I said, "but if I don't repeat it, then it doesn't count."

It's late, ten o'clock. Aunt Clara and I are the only ones up. She's in the rocker by the fire, mending a pair of trousers. I'm next to her, leaning onto the hearth to write this in the light. When she asked what I was writing, I said, "Oh, nothing." She just smiled, that's all.

November 8

The men in Uncle Henry's store were having a loud discussion. It seems that many of the non-Mormon shopkeepers have closed up and moved north, to the railroad town of Corinne. It's just a few miles from the Great Salt Lake.

"Why?" Pete had asked.

He received a chorus of answers. Some said Mormons are refusing to do business with Gentiles — that's what they call us non-Mormons, those who don't believe the way they do.

"They want this city to be theirs and theirs alone," said one man. "That's why they moved here from Illinois twenty years ago, don't you know."

But Uncle Henry said, "Brigham Young and I have been friends for years. He's always crossed the street to shake my hand."

"Why, then," said a man stoking the fire, "ain't there no customers here for the past weeks, you tell me why, Henry."

What I heard next made me feel sick inside. Father and Pete told the men they had walked the streets for three days, trying to get store owners to buy ads for their newspaper.

" 'No, thanks,' was the answer," Pete said. "They already advertise in the *Deseret News,* that's put out by the Mormons."

I worry that Mother will be furious. Father's dream of making money from publishing his own paper is not turning out like he'd planned. It all seemed to make sense when he was talking about it in Denver, but he didn't know the folks in railroad towns wouldn't pay their bills, and he didn't know his war wounds would make him need to rest. And now that we're in Salt Lake, he is surprised to learn we are outsiders.

In the front window there's a display of washboards. As I dusted them I heard Pete's voice. He said, "Sterling, don't worry. We'll find a way to make things work."

Before bed

I have just come from cleaning the kitchen. While I was wiping off the stove Pete strolled in through the front door, set a little bag of peppermints on the table, then walked out the back door. He didn't say a word! I've tucked the bag under my pillow because it smells so good and reminds me of him.

November 19
Still in Salt Lake City

The streets and rooftops and bare trees are covered with snow — it's so beautiful. People walk along the sidewalks in coats and scarves, women wear bonnets trimmed in fur. We can hear sleigh bells coming and going.

Although the weather is cold Father is doing well. He helps Uncle Henry in the store and every day he visits the editor of the *Utah Daily News*. Sometimes he helps set type. Sometimes he goes to the telegraph office to listen for news. One afternoon he listened to a reporter tap messages to another reporter at the *Chicago Tribune*. For half an hour clicking went back and forth, as if the two men were in the same room talking to each other.

Joe and our cousin Thomas keep each other entertained, but today there was a scuffle. They argued about who won a game of dominoes and began fighting. Somehow, one shoved the other, and Joe fell against the hot stove. His sleeve stuck against the side and the wool began to melt. I'm happy he wasn't burned, but the sleeve of his sweater has a huge scorch mark.

November 22

Yesterday Father hurried into the kitchen just as we were all sitting down to supper. "Shocking news about the Freeman brothers," he said. He was so out of breath it took him a few minutes to tell the story.

Just a few days ago there was trouble in a railroad town because of the Freemans. One of their editorials against gambling made everyone so mad there was a riot. The brothers also wrote cruel things about General Grant, President Lincoln, and Negroes in general. A mob wrecked the newspaper office and set it on fire. Their Washington Hand Press was destroyed along with all the type and other equipment. The brothers escaped and have fled back East.

"Apparently outlaws burned the town's jail and killed fourteen railroad workers," Father said. "I can't believe it. Just because they didn't like the editors' opinions. Thank God we weren't there." He put his hand on Mother's.

I bet she is thinking, *Thank God Father hasn't written any stupid editorials.*

December 1

This morning I heard the men in Uncle Henry's store arguing about Indians. A few days ago Lieutenant Colonel George Armstrong Custer and the Seventh Cavalry attacked some Cheyenne during a heavy snow-storm. This was Chief Black Kettle's camp on the upper Washita River. The horrible part is that the soldiers attacked before dawn. They killed women, children, and old men who had been sleeping.

I wondered if this was General Sherman's idea, but the men said, no, General Custer had acted on his own. It was part of the army's winter campaign against Indians.

December 4

Uncle Henry brought something to the house that's been in his store window for months. Since no one has bought it he's giving it to Aunt Clara for an early Christmas present.

Pete helped him carry it to their back porch. To me, it just looked like a barrel sawed in half with a washboard nailed to the side. It looked ridiculous and I said so.

"Libby," Uncle Henry replied, "this is a new invention. A Universal Clothes Wringer and, lookee here, there are double gears and a hand crank to make wash day easier."

Ellie and Mrs. Rowe came over to do wash and help with ours. We were excited to see a machine do something new. The old-fashioned way, Mother would pull a dripping shirt from the bucket and wring it out herself.

By the end of the day her hands would be red and so sore she could hardly make supper.

Now we ladies (sometimes I like to think of myself as a lady) crowded on the cold back porch and watched Aunt Clara. She held up a dripping dish towel and gently fed it between the wringer's metal teeth.

"All right, Libby." She nodded to me. I grabbed the long handle and began cranking it slowly, and slowly the teeth pressed down on the towel, pulling it through, squeezing water out as I turned the handle.

"Amazing," said Aunt Clara.

We spent the morning wringing out our clothes the modern way, taking turns in the kitchen to warm ourselves by the stove. But Ellie and I noticed a problem. The floor of the porch was littered with buttons. I examined them as we picked them up. They were from all the shirts, trousers, and pinafores we'd just washed.

The wringer was getting the water out, but it was also ripping off buttons as the material squeezed through the teeth. We showed Mother. She jingled the buttons in her palm then looked at Mrs. Rowe and Aunt Clara.

"Well," she said, "two things are obvious. One, we've just made more work for ourselves. Two, I don't think this machine was invented by a woman."

After we hung clothes around the house to dry, we put the kettle on for tea and scooped fresh butter from the churn. We sat at the benches around the table, then sliced a loaf of yesterday's bread. While we were eating in the warm kitchen we took a vote. It was *unanimous* (I had to look that up). We would rather wring clothes the old-fashioned way than sew on buttons again and again and again.

Aunt Clara opened a lid in her stove and dropped in a piece of firewood. "Come spring," she said, "that barrel will make a nice planter for my flowers."

December 23
Still in Salt Lake City

I've had a bad cold, so have not felt like writing. Today is the first time in two weeks that I've been able to walk to the kitchen without coughing.

There's still snow on the ground and as I look out the window I can see that it has begun to snow again. In the mountains above us there have been blizzards all week. Two railroad men who braved the storm to come down for provisions told Uncle Henry that tall snow fences built last year are completely buried. Also, the temperature inside the Wasatch Hotel was five degrees below zero. *Inside.*

Work on the railroad keeps stopping because of bad weather. Father said Casement's Army is spread out for nearly 150 miles, from surveyors to graders to tracklayers.

"Spread out like beads on a necklace," he said. "The Great Race is still on, but it may be spring before Union Pacific makes real progress."

Christmas Eve

When I write Kate and Annie, they won't believe what I'm about to say here.

This morning my cousin Jimmy arrived from Idaho Territory on horseback. His wife's horse pulled a type of sled with their tent and other belongings. What surprised me into silence was Jimmy's wife is an Indian! Her name is Nahanee and hanging from the pommel of her saddle was a cradle board with a papoose inside. Their baby has dark brown eyes, black hair, and his name is Little Bear Spoon. Nahanee and Little Bear are the first Indians I've ever seen.

Jimmy looks like a mountain man. His hair, light

brown, falls just below his shoulders. He wears a buck-skin jacket with fringe under the sleeves, and denim trousers tucked into knee-high moccasins. Jimmy is very tender to his wife and son.

Later

It's five o'clock Christmas morning and I'm writing this quickly. Aunt Clara is making coffee and preparing cinnamon cakes. The ham is spiked with cloves and soaking in honey, ready to roast.

I've now met all my girl cousins who have been drop-ping in and out over the last few days with their hus-bands and children. Jimmy is the only one who married an Indian, but everyone treats her fine. Nahanee and Little Bear are family and that's all there is to it.

Nahanee is nice to me — she gave me some red yarn. Now my braids are tied at the ends like hers. I have trouble understanding her English, but we get along well even so. She speaks to Jimmy and their baby in Shoshoni, her native language. I enjoy watching her because she is so like any other mother with a baby that I forget she's an Indian.

Nahanee has just come in from the backyard where

they slept in their tipi, next to Pete's tent. She put Little Bear on the rug in front of the fire. He's only a few months old so he lies on his back and tries to grab his feet. His moccasins have white-and-red beadwork around the ankle.

Must help Aunt Clara now.

January 1, 1869

Everyone talks about New Year's Resolutions so Ellie and I made three.

1. not to gossip
2. try to think the best of people
3. not to be nosy

Oh, Christmas was wonderfully busy. Ellie and Mrs. Rowe arrived with a basket of fresh bread from one of the bakeries. I was so happy they came. Also, I loved meeting my many relatives and holding all their babies. Four of Jimmy's sisters are what's called "plural wives." This means they married Mormon men who already had at least one other wife. This seems a lonely thing, to share a husband. I was more shocked and disappointed about this than I was about Nahanee. (Truly, I was thrilled about Nahanee.)

January 18

Already I have broken my resolutions. First, I told Ellie my opinion on plural wives and got so carried away I found myself shouting, in fact, I came close to swooning. I wasn't thinking the best of my cousins and I was gossiping. Then I was nosy, but this I couldn't help.

Ellie and I were taking Father his lunch pail at the *Daily News* where he's been working the press. On our way back we passed Brigham Young's block. Out front there were two girls rolling a hoop down the street. It was sunny and not too cold, so we stopped.

"May we visit with you?" I asked. The girls looked at each other, then the older one said, "Father said we're not to mingle with Gentiles."

"It's all right," Ellie said, "we're just girls, like you."

The four of us stood there a moment, then the older one ran toward the gate. She peeked inside, then motioned for us to follow.

"Wait there," she whispered, pointing to a bench below a window. She disappeared into a door of the house.

The younger girl stood on the bench to look inside, her face against the glass. I did the same, so did Ellie. To our surprise we were looking in at a well-stocked general store. In Brigham Young's house!

"All our aunties have credit here," the girl told us, "so we never go without things we need." On the polished wooden counter there were large square jars full of candy, and there was a chocolate cake under glass. The shelves had bolts of calico, ribbons, teacups, and other household items. I saw baskets of apples and onions, also barrels of beans. A man was behind the counter, handing something to the girl.

When she came outside she smiled at us. "Here," she said, giving us each a tiny piece of cloth about two inches square. There was a strong, pleasant smell of cinnamon.

"Thank you," I said, "but what is this?"

"Look." With her fingers she unraveled a thread from my cloth and put it in her mouth. "You do it."

"It's our favorite treat," the younger girl said. "The man puts drops of cinnamon oil on it, and we can chew the ravelings all day long. Spit them out when the flavor's gone."

I think Brigham Young's daughters wanted to be friends, but that was the last time we saw them. The next day Father announced we were leaving Salt Lake City to rejoin the railroad camps.

February 1

We are on the road again, camped near Ogden, about 40 miles north of Salt Lake City. We can see some of the graders and tracklayers who have worked their way down through Weber Canyon.

About our newspaper. One morning last week, Father woke up and said he was selling our Washington Hand Press to the *Daily News*. Mother smiled and didn't say a word. Pete didn't look too disappointed, either.

"I can't make enough money with it," Father said. "The editor will pay me $40 for everything — that'll take care of us for a while."

When Father and Pete went to Uncle Henry's shed where the press had been stored, they discovered something that was to delay our trip for three days. Somehow two boys playing (that's right, Joe and Thomas) had knocked down a shelf that held the boxes of type. Littered on the cold dirt were hundreds of tiny letters from *A* to *Z*. My brother and cousin weren't spanked, but they did have to return every single letter to its proper box. This meant they had to pick up each one, examine it backwards, then brush off the dirt that stuck to its ink.

It took them hours and hours. When they came in the house for a sandwich and to warm themselves I said, "Be sure to mind your p's and q's, ha-ha." They didn't laugh.

"Libby," Mother said, "since you know so much you can help them."

I was mad all day. Mad at myself. I wish I could learn not to say everything that comes into my mind. I don't know the whole story about the Freeman brothers, but I hope I'm never run out of town for my careless words.

February 3

Joe is missing! There's a frantic search, that's all I can say right now. Except, oh God, it's my fault.

+= =+

Later

I'm in the tent to change into warmer clothes so will quickly write some more.

After breakfast Joe and I stayed in camp while everyone else rode to town for supplies. Joe was reading in our tent, and I was outside by the fire. An hour passed. Needing to stretch I went to ask Joe if he'd like to walk with me. When I opened the flap I was shocked to see he wasn't reading his sailing book at all. It was my diary, *this* diary!

I flew at him screaming, "Get out! I never want to see you again!" and other cruel words I now regret. For many minutes I suffered on my cot, holding this book to my chest, wondering what secrets of mine he'd read. I'd forgotten I left it on top of my trunk this morning, so he must have seen it there. (Would I have resisted reading *his* diary if he had one?) Finally I calmed down enough to face him, but when I came out of our tent, he was not in sight.

"Joe," I called, again and again. There are other campsites nearby so I ran to each one, calling his name, asking if anyone had seen a little brown-haired boy in suspenders. No one had. By the time Mother and everyone drove up in the wagon two hours had passed.

Pete and Father are on horseback, searching, calling. I'm just sick with worry. Why wasn't I more patient with him?

It's almost suppertime. Mother is hysterical and cannot think about cooking. I have never seen her so worried, now especially because the sun is about to set, which means the air will quickly freeze. "What was Joe wearing?" she keeps asking me. I've confessed my part in Joe's running off, and have been consoled by everyone.

"Libby," said Mother, "he's such a fearless boy and such a responsibility. I don't blame you for being so angry with him."

Later still

At sundown Father and Pete came back for warmer coats and to light torches. Pete looked at his watch, then closed it without saying what time it was. I ran to him and grabbed his arm, not caring what he thought of me.

"Please find my brother, please . . ." but a sob choked me and I could say no more. Pete pulled me into his arms and held me tight, as he would a sister. Then he climbed into his saddle. Someone handed him a flaming torch, one to Father also, then they rode off with several other men.

For a long time Ellie and I watched the row of lights move into the black distance.

Near midnight

We still wait. Mother has collapsed on her cot, exhausted. Mrs. Rowe and Ellie take turns sitting with her. I pace outside in the cold air, my cloak thin comfort.

Before sunrise

Did not sleep. In the gray morning light we can see horses coming this way. Have they found Joe? we wonder. Why doesn't someone ride ahead with news for us?

Later

As the horsemen drew closer I started to run toward them. Ellie ran, too. I recognized Father and saw that he was carrying something in his arms. "Is it Joe?" I cried to Ellie, unable to run further. We held each other, waiting.

Finally, one horseman broke into a gallop toward us. Pete! And he was smiling.

Two days later

I write this in Ellie's tent while we wait out a snow-storm (in our comfortable trousers). About Joe's safe return: All of us were overjoyed. Mother wrapped him in wool blankets and sat with him in front of the fire. Joe was too sleepy to make much sense, but Father said they found him a couple miles away, at the hot springs, lying in a crevice protected from the wind and cold. How he got there we don't know exactly, but it seems when he fled our campsite after I yelled at him, an old farmer gave him a ride in his wagon, believing Joe was running *to* someplace, not *from*.

I have hugged my brother so many times now he's probably sick of me, but I'm so relieved he's home. I'm trying hard to forgive him for reading my secrets. Does he know about that night in Hell Town?

+≕ ≕+

February 10

Now that my terrible scare with Joe has passed, I'll try to pay attention to the other history being made. We've heard rumors that Chinese workers are north of the Great Salt Lake. Everyone is talking at once. Could these be Crocker's Pets, all the way from California? It seems as if the railroads are going to meet soon, but where? And when?

Other news is that Brigham Young is in Ogden. We saw him step down from a carriage that had been driven by a Negro man. Mr. Young wore a tall black hat and a Prince Albert cape, dark green. He walked with a cane, for style I think because he was not limping. Ellie and I think he's as dignified as any of the army generals we've seen.

Pete says that when Brigham Young found out the tracks wouldn't go through his city he was furious. So he's just going to build his own narrow-gauge railroad to connect Ogden with Salt Lake City. Meanwhile he and some Mormon bishops have contracts with Union Pacific *and* Central Pacific to help hurry up the work. The sooner the rails are joined, the sooner trains will come into the Mormon capital.

Later

Have decided New Year's resolutions are utterly ridiculous. How do I know what tomorrow will bring? I think when I get up each morning I will ask God to help me be kind and gentle, especially to my little brother. If by bedtime I've failed, then I'll just try again the next day.

February 15
Still in Ogden

The countryside is white with snow. It's beautiful, but camping is not fun in the winter. My feet are wet all the time and it's tiring to be out in the cold. I wish I were back in Uncle Henry's nice home, the three months we were there went too fast.

Because we're near a schoolhouse, Ellie, Joe, and I spend the day there to keep warm, but also to learn. There are 12 other students, ages five to fourteen (I'm the eldest). Our teacher, Miss Belle, is sixteen years old and is strict, very strict, with spelling and grammar. I'm glad Father didn't sell our dictionary.

February 17

Blizzards for three days. Father has moved us all to Mrs. Buffington's Boarding House in downtown Ogden, so Ellie and I share a cozy room in the attic with three other young ladies.

Ogden has wide streets like Salt Lake City and neat, trim houses with orchards fed by mountain streams. It, too, was settled by Mormons. The telegraph office is one block away from where we're staying. Father goes there to sort through and read telegrams, then he wires his own stories to Denver. News from the Wasatch is that tracks somewhere between the tunnels have buckled because they were laid on frozen ground. A derailment has slowed up work there again.

"I knew it was dangerous," Mother said. "Folks who work too fast often make mistakes."

Work also has slowed down with Central Pacific. There's been an outbreak of cholera and whole crews — Chinese and whites — are too sick to work.

Every night at supper we eat at a long table in the parlor, with other men and ladies who board here. We children are allowed to eat with the adults as long as we don't say a word (this is hard for me!). Last evening all the adults seemed to talk at once.

"A costly mistake is being made," one of the men said, passing a platter of meat to Father. Father said, "I agree, you're absolutely right."

It seems that just north of the Great Salt Lake our Union Pacific crews have begun work on a trestle heading west. This tall wooden bridge is not the problem, though. The problem is that just 100 yards away, the Chinese crews are crossing the very same gorge, but going the other way! Instead of meeting up with our bridge, they're building their own by filling the gorge with dirt.

"This makes no sense at all," Mother said.

"No, ma'am, it surely doesn't."

A bowl of roasted red potatoes was being handed around the table, followed by gravy urns, then corn, then green beans. Five loaves of bread were in the center of the table with plates of butter and jams. Everyone was saying "please" and "excuse me" and "thank you" while eating and passing things around. Mrs. Buffington stood proudly nearby to make sure there was enough food.

"Union Pacific and Central Pacific are so close they

can share each other's lunches," said another man. "Why don't the foremen just shake hands and get the job done?"

When dinner was over, I got up to help Mrs. Buffington clear the table, and Ellie did, too. We aren't required to do this since our parents are paying guests, but I do like to help. Also, I feel nervous when everyone's talking about interesting things, but I'm not alowed to join in.

While I sliced the pies and served them on dessert plates, I formed my opinion, but will keep it here. The railroad bosses are greedy. Someone with common sense should have decided *months* ago where the tracks should meet. Someone who cares more about our country than about money in his pocket.

February 27

Pete and Father rode horses up north to see The Big Fill and The Big Trestle for themselves.

"It's such a waste," Father said when they returned days later. "The railroad beds are side by side, going in opposite directions. It's not the workers' fault — they're just doing what they're told."

Pete was mad, too. "If the bosses and shareholders

don't make a decision soon," he said, "the Chinese will end up in New York and we'll be camping on the beaches of California."

Father said we'll stay at this boarding house for now. "I don't want my family stranded out in the desert," he said, "while stubborn men twiddle their thumbs."

At breakfast this morning one of the guests, a reporter from *The Oregonian*, explained that the railroad stockholders are happy about this situation. They will earn land grants worth many thousands of dollars for each wasted mile, so the longer things go without a meeting place, the richer in land they'll be.

The reporter sipped his coffee, then shook his head with disgust. "No good ever comes from greed," he said. "Wise men know that the love of money is the root of all evil."

Then someone said, "Old Brigham is no better. He's got church members working on both sides of the railroad, so he'll profit nicely for as long as this continues."

"Here, here," said voices around the table.

+≒ ≒+

A fight broke out the other day. Union Pacific workers threw frozen dirt clods at the Chinese, called them terrible names, attacked with pickaxes, then set off explosions. Since several Chinese were killed, they (the Chinese) used dynamite. An avalanche of rocks buried several men alive and three mules were killed. Finally someone with authority ordered the men to stop fighting and make a truce.

Pete has taken odd jobs at Mrs. Buffington's to pay for his keep. He's busy all day, chopping firewood, raking the barn, and so forth — I admire him for working so hard. Father won't collect any pay for his stories until we get back to Denver, so we each have small jobs. I have no stomach for emptying spittoons and am dangerous with cooking, so instead my duties are to set and clear the table for each meal in exchange for food. Joe brings wood into the kitchen morning and evening, also Mother helps wash linens and such three afternoons a week. Mrs. Rowe and Ellie pitch in but will take no pay — they just like to help and to keep busy. (We're all thankful that Mrs. Buffington does *not* have a Universal Clothes Wringer.)

The other day before washing, I found the little piece of cloth from Brigham Young's daughter in my pocket. It still had a good cinnamon smell, but I've not unraveled it for chewing. Instead, I've tucked it inside the front pages of this diary.

Miss Belle drills us and drills us on spelling. It seems a bother to me, but she says good spelling is *essential* to good *communication*. (I had to look up both these words.)

After supper some of the guests gather in the front room where there's a warm stove and several kerosene lamps. People read newspapers or books. Pete has almost finished *A Tale of Two Cities*. Sometimes when he turns a page he glances up at me, then smiles. (I know this because I am glancing at *him*!) Besides reading, there's always a game of checkers going and Joe is learning chess from Mr. Buffington, in fact they play every night. Last night Joe beat a reporter from *The Boston Journal* who was so mad that he lost to a kid, he stormed out to the porch and knocked down a chair.

Joe's only seven. I think he's very clever to have learned so fast. Also, he's already on page 198 of *Two Years Before the Mast*. He's confided to me that he wants to be a sailor like Father was, but I've not told Mother about this.

Later

Mr. Russell the photographer stayed two nights and at breakfast this morning he sat next to me. When he reached for the jug of syrup that was in front of us, I could smell chemicals on his sleeve.

Later, after chores, Joe and I saw him by his wagon where he was developing his photographic plates. His beard had been freshly barbered and the way he smiled at us I knew he liked children. He let us touch his camera. The wood is heavy and smooth. He showed us some of his pictures, then he very carefully lifted a glass negative from a crate — it was as large as a windowpane. When he drove off that afternoon he waved good-bye to us, his little black wagon rattling with his bottles of powder, mixer, and other chemicals.

When I came up to the attic tonight, I noticed a thin bouquet of dried flowers on my trunk, two daisies and a rose. No card or message. When I touched them and caught the faint scent of peppermint, my heart began to race. Could this be from Pete?

I close my journal tonight daring to feel happy, daring to think Pete might care for me.

March 5
Still in Ogden

Yesterday Ulysses S. Grant was sworn in as President of the United States. I wish I'd had a chance to speak with him last summer, either at the Laramie Hotel or Fort Sanders, because right now my most vivid memory of our new president is that he stubbed out his cigar in his teacup.

March 6

I'm glad someone's in charge! On the very day Mr. Grant became president he scolded the railroad companies. He said if they don't agree on a meeting place immediately, the government will not pay them.

"Bravo," said Mother. "I guess Mr. Grant has more character than I'd thought." Father said, "Here, here. Another president with backbone, thank God."

After supper Pete came up to me in the reading room. "Miss Libby," he said, "there's a fair breeze blowing, would you like to take a walk?"

To myself I thought, *Oh, yes!* but to him I replied, "Hm . . . well . . . all right . . . I guess so."

Wind was coming from the north, so I pulled my shawl tight, my braids tucked inside down my back. There was no moon yet, just pricks of starlight against the black sky. The Wasatch Mountains seemed so close they blocked the eastern sky like a wall. Somewhere up there men were warming themselves around campfires, getting ready to sleep on the work train. They were almost finished laying rails through the tunnels.

When Pete touched my face with his hand, I was too surprised to speak. "Miss Libby, you surely smell good." Suddenly he leaned forward and kissed my cheek, then he reached into his vest pocket to pull out his watch.

"My!" he said, "it's nearly ten o'clock, we should get back."

I am writing this quickly before bed, one little candle on the sill is all the light I have. Ellie's cot is under the other window — I think she's asleep so will wait until tomorrow to tell her about Pete. I wish she were awake! There's so much fluttering going through my heart and mind, I wonder if I'm in love????

+═══ ═══+

March 7

When Pete smiled at me during breakfast, my face felt so hot I could hardly swallow. Ellie noticed, of course. As she and I carried dishes into the kitchen she whispered, "Tell me!"

So after we helped put things back in the pantry, we hung up our aprons by the back door and hurried outside.

"He kissed you?" she nearly shouted after I told her. "Oh, Libby, did you swoon? *I* would have. Then what happened? Tell me everything. I promise not to breathe a word."

We walked for an hour along one of the creeks that flows down from the mountains. Overhead the poplars were beginning to blossom, and the air was warm with the promise of spring. I felt so happy to have Ellie as my friend, with something special to tell her.

Later

After supper a man in the reading room handed me his copy of the *Utah Daily News*. "Young lady," he said, leaning back in his chair to light his pipe, "you remind me of my daughter. Tell me what you think of this Great Race."

I was so thrilled he asked my opinion that I just said, "Oh!" and began to quickly read the front page. The story described the grading camps as having "the appearance of a mighty army. As far as the eye can see is a continuous line of tents, wagons, and workers."

"I wish I could be there right now," I said. I told the man that I know we're in a race, but it hardly feels like it when I'm sitting in a parlor drinking tea. I want to *see* the rails actually moving forward.

"Me, too," he said, holding a match over the bowl of his pipe.

We discussed other parts of the story. Suddenly I felt brave, and answered all his questions. Really I don't know a lot, but it was wonderful to be asked my opinion by someone ready to listen.

March 15

On the move again! We ladies had tearful good-byes with Mrs. Buffington, who packed us a lunch of beef pies, hard-boiled eggs, cookies, and jars of lemonade. She stood on the porch and waved with her handkerchief.

After one month together day in and day out, we'd become good friends.

Am writing by firelight, after drying the supper dishes. We're now camped by the hot springs north of Ogden, where Joe spent the night when he was lost. I love the way steam rises from the pools, making a thick white cloud that can be seen for miles.

Yesterday we hiked there and took a good long soak. I wore my old cotton dress with bloomers, because it's not proper to go naked (though I think it would feel divine). Ellie practiced her swoon once and only once, for the water was much too hot to go completely under and there's a stink of sulphur she didn't want to get in her hair.

The noise from the "Town on Wheels" is loud even from far across the new tracks. I wish it were far enough away that I couldn't hear a sound, so bothered am I by the memory of that night.

We are close enough to the work train that we can smell the good aroma of bacon and eggs and fresh bread. This morning after breakfast Miss Sallie, the Irish cook, brought us a wooden bucket half filled with left-over coffee. Mother said, "Thank you very much, Miss Sallie." Pete scooped his cup in, but stopped. We all looked. Floating on top were bits of bread and other little things that appeared to be chewed food.

"Mercy," said Mother as she poured it into the dirt.

Father told us that he peeked into the dining car the other evening while the first shift of workers ate supper. With their forks they helped themselves to platters of meat and bread. Buckets of hot coffee were on the table, so the men just leaned forward and dipped in their cups.

"Guess that explains the seasonings on top," Father laughed. But Mother didn't smile. I still haven't told her how Miss Sallie cleans the plates.

March 23

The "rolling factory" moves forward every day. Father and Pete are now friends with the men in the telegraph car because they visit so often. They said the telegraph clicks all day long now as newspapers around the country ask for updates. There's excitement in the air. By this I mean everyone talking about the railroad speaks quickly, almost out of breath. Horsemen ride back and forth from the railroad to report on each mile moved westward.

Sightseers from across the territory arrive daily with tents and families, as the important day draws near. Mother and Mrs. Rowe are happy to see other ladies of good moral character. Our tents look like a holiday campground. Laundry is strung here and there and many of us have American flags hanging from poles. In the distance is Union Pacific's herd of cattle — the cowboys stay near them with their own campfires and chuckwagon.

Further south is the "Town on Wheels," pulling up stakes, packing wagons, and hauling their wares to be closer to the workers. Noise from their brawls and wild living is the only blemish on this adventure.

I need to write Kate and Annie, so will close now.

March 26

Indians are camped on the northern horizon! We can see tipis and horses. Someone said they're Shoshoni from Chief Washakie's people in Idaho Territory. They often come to Salt Lake City to trade. If Jimmy and Nahanee are with them I hope we can see one another again. People also say that Gosiutes are nearby, but we've not seen them.

This morning I rode in the wagon with Joe to help with his job because he has a bad cold. As I carried the pail I felt awkward — there were no other girls in sight! I tried not to stare at the men as they dipped their cups into the water, but it was hard not to. One of the mule whackers quickly put on his shirt before approaching me, then said, "Thank you, miss" after he drank.

When they all returned to work I sat in the wagon and watched what looked like a man dancing! Father called him a "gandy dancer" and explained he was actually balancing himself on the long handle of a shovel, like someone walking a tightrope. The shovel was lifting a rail a few inches off the ground so another man could push gravel underneath. This made things level.

How all these men know what to do, when they do, still seems to me like a beautiful ballet. And now I have a favorite, the "gandy dancer."

Last year when I was in Denver, sitting comfortably in our kitchen, I never dreamed I'd know anything about railroad men or that I'd have an Indian relative and cousins who are polygamists. My mind feels stretched!

April 7

We've been camped in Corinne for the past week, ahead of the tracklayers, to wait for the work train to catch up. And today it did!

Near noon we heard the whistle shriek and saw the engine's big white cloud of steam. From here the tracks will go west, toward the sunset, toward meeting Central Pacific.

The engineer let Joe climb up into the cab. First Joe rang the brass bell by pulling its string about twenty times. He waved to us from the window, then he leaned out to spit. "Hey, Libby," he yelled, still waving, "how about that man-sized spit?"

Corinne is not the pretty town I imagined. It's just tents and shanties. Lots of eating houses offer meals for 50 cents and among the saloons there's one sign of civilization: the Corinne Book Store. When Pete saw there were books, he hiked through the sagebrush to the small shack. An hour later he returned to our campsite carrying a parcel which, to my surprise, he handed to me.

"It's brand new, just published," he said, rolling his hands so I would open it faster.

I pulled apart the brown paper and read the title. "*Little Women*, by Louisa May Alcott. Thank you. But why . . . ?"

He smiled, then threw his hands in the air. "I just wanted to get you something, Libby."

At that moment I felt so happy, if Mother hadn't been standing there I think I might have kissed him.

Now in our tent. Everyone's asleep so I'll write fast — my candle is as short as a nickel and beginning to sputter.

I carried *Little Women* with me all day, reading every chance I could. It's a handsome book, 546 pages and 42 chapters. The exact middle page is page 273. I wonder how long it will take me to get there. Oh, I love the story, it's about four sisters!

Candle is going. . . .

April 8

Another train pulled into town and was switched to a sidetrack. Out jumped dozens of soldiers from the 21st Infantry, including the army band. They played victory songs and marches, such stirring music Mother and Mrs. Rowe and the other ladies cried with happiness. Ellie and I were so excited by the train whistles and bell, and by the trumpets and drum, we swung our arms and marched along the tracks. It was *exhilarating* (had to look that up).

It has been sunny, but the air is chilled. I wear my cloak buttoned up over my dress, and my wool leggings. My bonnet is such a nuisance I leave it in our tent. Ellie had a birthday last week, she's fourteen. Her mother gave her a beautiful new dress that she sewed from cloth bought at Uncle Henry's. It is dark brown with red piping along the neck and sleeves. Her lace bloomers show just a bit below her hem. I think she looks lovely.

Since Mr. Rowe is still further ahead with the surveyors, he had a messenger on a fast pony bring a package to Ellie. Inside was a beautiful string of blue beads with silver dimes spaced every few inches. It is the most interesting necklace I've ever seen. She's very pleased with this birthday present.

I'm starting chapter two of *Little Women*. After lunch Ellie and I climbed into the back of our wagon where it was warm out of the wind, and I read 12 pages out loud. We both wish we had several sisters.

April 11

Finally! Word came over the telegraph that the tracks will meet at Promontory Summit. The railroad bosses were up all last night and at last made a decision, a whole month after President Grant ordered them to do so.

The 21st Infantry marched to Central Pacific's rail-head. It took them two days to go 50 miles. They will board a little train there that will take them to San Francisco. Father said that it used to be when the army changed stations from East to West it took them several months to get across the territories.

Every time I think of Pete buying me that new book, I feel soft inside. I do wish he'd ask me to go for a walk with him — the evenings are lovely, and, oh, the stars! They're so brilliant I would gaze at them all night if I could stay awake.

April 17

Today is my birthday. Mrs. Rowe and Mother baked a cake in our Dutch oven and iced it with melted chocolate bars Uncle Henry had given us. I'm happy to be another year older.

Because I'm now fifteen Mother brushed out my braids, then twirled and pinned my hair on top of my head. She gave me two of her small ivory combs and showed me how to place them in my bun just so.

When Pete saw my new lady look, he put his hands in his pockets and leaned against the wagon. "I do declare," he said. "Libby, you are as pretty as the day."

I should have thanked him for the compliment, but I just looked at his face. It dawned on me with growing pleasure that, for some days now, Pete has been saying my name, just plain Libby. I like that.

April 23

Our campsite is just north of the Great Salt Lake and nearby there are salt marshes with all types of water birds and seagulls. The sky is a beautiful cerulean blue.

Hearing the gulls reminds me of the harbor at New York. I was five years old when we lived there, but I do remember fishing boats and birds circling overhead. It seems funny to be in the middle of the desert and to hear cries of birds that belong along the seacoast.

Everyone's talking about a new invention called the Westinghouse "airbrake." It means the engineer himself will be able to slow down the train from levers inside his locomotive, and there won't need to be brakemen anymore standing on the roof of each car. Father said it might take years, though, for all the trains to have them.

"Trains are getting safer," said Mother, "but I just pray that tracks and bridges are, too."

April 27

Now we're in Junction City, some miles west of Corinne. The town is larger and more lively. We can see the grading camps clear to the Promontory Mountains and it does indeed look like a mighty army. We can hear explosions from the black powder used to blast through the rocks.

Ellie and I want to take Joe up close but Father said it's too dangerous. A man was killed yesterday, blown up into the air because he didn't run from the blast in time. Others were badly wounded by flying stones.

We see freight wagons drive back and forth between Union Pacific and Central Pacific railheads, with messages and supplies. Their runs are becoming shorter because each side moves forward three to four miles a day.

It feels like the Great Race is nearing its end because Promontory Summit is just 10 miles away. But still there are three trestles to be built and more railbeds must be carved from the rocks. Crews work from sunrise until sundown. Now that winter is over the days are getting longer, though the extra sunlight hasn't yet warmed the earth. The desert is still a cold place in the spring.

April 29

I saw two Chinese men today! They were hurrying with poles over their shoulders that had water pails on each end. They wore dark blue cotton pants, loose shirts, and wide-brimmed hats. I was as excited to see them as I was to meet Nahanee and Little Bear.

A contest took place yesterday that I wish with all my heart I could have witnessed. On the other side of the Summit, Central Pacific's crew of ironmen, tracklayers, spikers, tampers, and hundreds of other men all worked together as fast as they could. Instead of walking with their equipment they ran, the tracks moving forward nearly one mile each hour. Their goal was to lay 10 miles of track in one day.

The men began after breakfast. During the middle of the day they stopped for one hour to rest, then when the sky was growing dark again, they lay down their tools in exhaustion. In 12 hours they had gone 10 miles and 56 feet, a new record. Where they started is named Camp Victory.

Mr. Crocker had handpicked his best crew and promised to pay each of them four days' wages for one day's work. He wanted to show that his railroad crew was superior to ours, but in my opinion, it was an unfair contest. Unfair, because we were 9 miles from the end, so there weren't even 10 left for us to try. I'm mad that we didn't have an honest chance to win. (Funny, I feel as if Union Pacific is my own railroad.)

After supper

A wagon train of 16 families from eastern Utah is camped nearby. Father and I talked to one of the men last night at their campfire. He told us they came through Echo Canyon and are now going around the north end of the Great Salt Lake. From there they'll take the California Trail to Sacramento. They're hurrying to get over Donner Pass before snows fall.

Father said, "If you stay with us a couple weeks, trains will be coming through and can carry you all the way to California."

The man was quiet. He looked at the covered wagons drawn in a circle around his campfire. "That's a good idea," he said, "but everyone here wants to keep moving fast as we can."

The travelers left at sunrise this morning. I woke up to their bugle call. I could see their oxen slowly pulling onto the trail, their breaths steamed in the cold air. There was a rattle of pans and pots, the creak of wheels, then they were gone, just a spot of dust on the horizon.

May 1, 1869
Promontory Summit

We're here! Men from Union Pacific are laying down a section of sidetrack to be ready when the rest of the tracklayers catch up. Families such as ours are camped at a safe distance from the wild "Town on Wheels." (Father and everyone else we know still call it "Hell on Wheels.")

Everyone waits.

Ellie and I met some children who came all the way from California on Central Pacific's work train. Their father, Mr. Jim Strobridge, is the big boss overseeing all the work and because he wanted his family to travel with him, he built a special boxcar that is like a rolling house. Mrs. Strobridge even has a front porch with an awning and a canary cage hanging out front.

Joe asked one of the girls why her father wears a patch over one eye. We learned that in the Sierra Nevada mountain range, Mr. Strobridge got too close to some nitroglycerin and the explosion put out his eye. She also told us that dozens of Chinese were buried in avalanches and their bodies can't be dug out until after the snows melt.

Today Central Pacific's tracks reached the Summit. (I wonder if this means they won the race?) Everyone waits now for Union Pacific to work its way toward us, up Promontory Mountain. I feel as if we're in the middle of a loud village. As far as we can see there are tents, hundreds and hundreds bunched in groups — the Chinese, Irish, and Mormons each have their own sections.

Father and Pete walked along these little campsites

and later told us that men have put up signs with names such as Deadfall, Murder Gulch, and Last Chance. When I said I was going to take a walk, Pete said, "Libby, don't go anywhere near those camps, they're too dangerous for a lady such as yourself."

I turned away so he wouldn't see my face. It felt as if I was blushing, but why? I puzzled over this all day, and now that it is evening and I'm about to blow out our lamp, it has come to me. I blush because Pete thinks of me as a lady. This pleases me.

May 3

We noticed that some of the tents put up days ago are already being taken down. Father said Central Pacific is sending workers back to California. A supply train will go with them so they can repair any tracks that had been built in haste.

It's cloudy and cold today. In the privacy of our tent I've been practicing brushing my hair up on top of my head. My arms get tired, and at moments I think it's a bother to be a lady. A net like Mother's seems easier, but I prefer the elegance of turned-up hair. Ellie has asked her mother if she, too, may wear her hair like mine, braids being so girlish now.

But Mrs. Rowe said, "When you are fifteen, Ellie, then you may dress like a lady."

May 5

Clouds are dark and heavy. The air smells like rain. I'm glad I didn't pack away my wool leggings, but now that my hair is up my neck feels cold!

We heard that a riot broke out at Camp Victory, between Chinese gangs. One man was killed. Father said it was because of a gambling debt, but I think everyone's restless. We are all waiting for Mr. Durant, who is the vice president of Union Pacific, and other officials to arrive, then we can say hooray and return to our homes.

I wonder if the Chinese will sail back to China or will they start new lives here? Father said they can become citizens only if they were born in this country.

This made me think of something. My cousin, Jimmy Spoon, is a citizen, but his wife, Nahanee, is not. Since their baby, Little Bear, is half Indian and half American, does that mean he's half a citizen? How can that be? I don't know, but I hope Ulysses S. Grant will figure this out now that he's President.

Am on page 129 of *Little Women*. Oh, how I identify with Josephine (I like her full name rather than just Jo). She has stomped about in a temper and said hateful things to her little sister that she later regretted. Also, same as me, she loves to write and is a dreadful cook. (I wish I had a sister like her!)

May 7

Late this afternoon our tracklayers arrived at the Summit! A Union Pacific engine came to a stop with a loud release of steam. Facing it on another sidetrack was a locomotive from California. Both engines greeted each other with a sharp whistle.

Finally. It was the first time trains from the Pacific coast and the Atlantic coast had met, and I saw it with my own eyes! We cheered with excitement, men threw their hats in the air, ladies waved handkerchiefs, and Joe ran wild with some other boys. One fellow proudly showed us the blackened sleeve of his shirt, which had three large holes. He'd gotten too close to one of the engines and the smokestack spit out cinders and soot that landed on him — I think this is almost as dangerous as putting coins on the track.

Everyone is still waiting for Mr. Durant and the others to arrive. Then workers will lay the final half mile — that's just about 2,500 feet.

May 8

Mr. Leland Stanford, the president of Central Pacific Railroad, arrived today from California aboard the locomotive *Jupiter* and I have never seen such a handsome train. The cowcatcher has been painted a brilliant blue, the wheels are bright red.

Mr. Russell and other photographers have been taking pictures, but I think it is a pity that when his photographs are printed, people will only see the *Jupiter* as black and gray.

It has been raining all morning and all afternoon, a miserable cold rain. Promontory Summit is a sea of sticky wet mud. Mr. Stanford is furious because he was expecting a big party when he arrived, but there'll be no celebration until Mr. Durant arrives from the East. What is taking so long?

At least five journalists got fed up with waiting and left for Salt Lake City. They'll write their stories when they read the telegrams. But I wonder how they're going to get the story exactly right if they don't see it for themselves, and what if they make a mistake?

"This is an important historic event," I said to Father.

"Libby," he answered, "journalists make mistakes all the time. Sometimes history is just lies that men have agreed upon."

I've considered Father's words, but I'm troubled by them. If what he says is true then a reporter could leave out certain details in his story or even make them up and readers would believe things happened exactly as written. Then years later those details will have become "history." In my opinion this is irresponsible.

I'm in our tent, trying to stay warm by the light of two kerosene lamps. It is still raining. Instead of washing dishes I've set them outside on the crate and am letting God do it. Mother and everyone else are in Mrs. Rowe's tent playing cards, so I have a chance to be by myself to write and to read. I'm on page 178 . . . oh, I hope Josephine's father won't die from his war illness!

Today telegrams reported that Union Pacific is late because the bosses on board are being held hostage in

Piedmont, Wyoming. (Mr. Stanford was really upset at this news.) What happened is this: Angry workers piled railroad ties on the tracks, forcing the train to stop, and they wouldn't let it come to Promontory until their wages were paid. Forty-eight hours dragged by. Finally, somehow, many thousands of dollars were rushed to Piedmont, the workers were paid, and Union Pacific is once again on its way.

The ceremony of joining the two railroads was to take place today. We all look toward the Wasatch, hoping for a glimpse of the train, but there's not even a puff of steam in the distance.

Later

An hour ago Joe rushed into the tent with muddy feet and breathless news. It seems that soon after Union Pacific's ambush, the train was again delayed, this time in Weber Canyon, just 13 miles from Ogden. Some pilings under the Devil's Gate Bridge were washed out by heavy rains. Even after some repairs, the engineer was so worried that the bridge would collapse, he insisted that the passengers get out and walk across. (I would have been terrified on that wobbly thing!) The empty coaches were then pushed to the other side and the engine was left behind because the bridge couldn't bear its weight.

A replacement engine from Ogden, *No. 119,* is on its way to rescue the stranded people.

Sunday, May 9

It is still raining, but Joe, Ellie, and I have been so restless we went on a hike with Father, through the sage and mud and beyond the soggy tent camps. I wore my bonnet to protect my hair, which had taken almost an hour this morning to fix.

I asked Father how the trains would return home since there's no roundhouse here for them to turn around. He pointed to an area where there are tracks in the shape of a giant *Y.* Somehow the engines can switch tracks here and change directions.

The rain made us feel cold so we returned to our tents soaking wet, yet happy to have been out and about. I noticed Father has been limping again, but if the dampness bothers his legs, he doesn't complain.

Before supper

Even in the rain today tracklayers finished, but left out one rail for the ceremony tomorrow. We are 690 miles from Sacramento and 1,086 from Omaha. Maybe Union Pacific won the race for the most track laid all together and maybe Central Pacific won for its "Ten Mile Day." I don't know. After all these months people seem to care that it was done, period, not how fast or who finished first.

Something interesting: I added the mileage 690 plus 1,086. Since it equals 1,776 and 1776 is the year our Declaration of Independence was signed, I was thrilled at the coincidence. I jumped up to tell Father, but he said it had been planned that way. Last month when the men in Washington were trying to chose a meeting place they figured out a symbolic total for the mileage and that was that.

I guess they had nothing better to do.

May 10

I woke in the middle of the night and realized the rain had stopped. A breeze pushed at the sides of our tent. At first light we dressed quickly and ate breakfast. All day my hair was on top of my head, but the bun was so loose I worried it would fall. (I'm still not sure how to use Mother's combs and pins.)

Engine *No. 119* with its bright red wheels rolled into Promontory at about ten-thirty this morning with some cheering and bugles, but mostly folks were thinking, "It's about time."

It was a thrill to see it and the *Jupiter* nose to nose with just one length of rail separating them. I don't want to be like the absent journalists who write stories about what they *think* happened, so I will report only what I saw with my own eyes. By the way, my new opinion is this: Gossip and rumors make a mess of history.

Anyway, an army officer raised a large flag. Father said it was an old one, probably from 1818, because there were only 20 stars. I did see and hear the military band from Fort Douglas, also a Mormon band from the Tenth Ward in Salt Lake City. The crowd was unruly and loud, but Ellie and I managed to push our way between some boys to watch the grand moment.

Some time after twelve o'clock noon Mr. Strobridge and another man carried the last wooden tie and lowered it into position. It looked as if holes had already been drilled into the tie, to make the final spikes go in easier.

Finally a preacher opened the ceremony by calling for prayer and did he pray! After one solid minute had passed, Ellie leaned over and said, "Some ladies swoon about now." We tried not to laugh, for we knew this was a serious occasion. The good reverend kept his head bowed for another full minute. (His neck looked bright red under his collar.) Did he know that only a few people could hear him, that men were growing restless and joking among themselves?

When "Amen" was finally shouted, the last spike was placed above the hole. Both Mr. Stanford and Mr. Durant, who'd recently enjoyed several glasses of whiskey, were given hammers. Father explained to me that telegraph wires were hooked onto the spike and the hammers. This way the actual blow would telegraph a signal across the lines coast to coast.

Looking a bit unsteady on their feet, Mr. Stanford and Mr. Durant raised the hammers above their heads while someone cried, "Three . . . two . . . one!"

Then an amazing thing. They both swung at the spike and they both missed! The crowd cheered. No one seemed to care that the railroad officials themselves were too drunk to finish the job properly except Mr. Strobridge. He stepped in to help, looking at the spike sideways because of the patch over his eye. Moments later the deed was done, but I couldn't tell if *he* hit the last spike or if it was a worker next to him, because some pushing men blocked my view.

Bands burst into music, train whistles blew, bells rang, and finally the crowd parted so Mr. Russell and other photographers could take pictures. At that moment some more men shoved their way in front of Ellie and me so history will not record our two faces.

I saw officials from Union Pacific and Central Pacific shake hands. Irish and Mormon workers climbed onto the trains and the locomotive engineers stood by the headlamps holding out bottles of ale and champagne. The *Jupiter* had several small American flags, a type I'd not seen before — the stars were in a circle instead of in rows. After the crowds thinned out, Ellie and I got up close and counted: 37 stars for 37 states.

The sight of these two handsome locomotives facing each other, their cowcatchers touching, is one I'll remember for the rest of my life. I'll tell my children that in the middle of a lonely desert I witnessed an *extraordinary* (had to look that up) event.

But the best came later. Time to blow out the lamp. More tomorrow.

May 11

Breakfast is finished and cleaned up. I'm writing this while Father and Pete ready the mules. Our wagon is packed, so is Ellie's. We're going to spend a few days in Ogden with Mrs. Buffington, then on to Salt Lake City to visit Uncle Henry and Aunt Clara. Passenger trains are now expected to run regularly, so sometime in June we'll go by railroad to Cheyenne, then home. Mother and Mrs. Rowe want to wait until then to make sure spring rains are over and that wobbly bridges have been made sturdy.

Ellie and I aren't sad about our journey ending because in Denver we'll be neighbors. Since it turns out that her house is just a couple miles from mine, we can walk back and forth, or maybe I'll ride Tipsy there. I'm excited that soon I'll be able to sleep in my own cozy bed and sit in our cheerful kitchen.

Last night the "Town on Wheels" was wild with gambling and fights. Father said that railroad men earn their money like horses, but spend it like asses.

Our family joined with others to celebrate . . . it's odd but people still don't know who actually drove in the final spike. Around our campfire two fiddlers and a boy with a drum played music that set feet to tapping. After an hour of this, Pete took my arm and led me away from the fire. Scattered around the dark countryside were flickers of fire from the remaining campsites. Tents in Promontory were brightly lit, but only history will tell if it will remain a town after everyone goes home.

I pulled my shawl closer around my neck against the chill. It took several minutes for my eyes to adjust to the darkness. The sky was black, and the stars seemed to wiggle the way leaves on a tree turn in a breeze.

When Pete took my hand I could see his face in the starlight. He kissed the tips of my fingers, then he drew me to him and kissed my lips . . . he kissed me! Oh! For a moment I thought I would swoon. We held each other. I wanted the night to last forever, but too soon we were walking back toward camp, my arm looped through his. Someday I'll be able to tell Pete about this wonderful, new feeling washing over me: I love him, I'm certain of it.

Now it is morning. Mother is calling that all is ready so I must hurry this diary into my things. Joe will ride on the seat between her and Father. And I will walk with Pete.

My thoughts are full of wonder. I've just witnessed what everyone says is the greatest event in America's history, yet all I can think about are the small, good things: Father isn't limping as badly, Mother is cheerful, and Joe survived all his mischief; I have a new friend in Ellie and friends waiting for me in Denver.

Then there's my quietest, tiniest, most favorite thought for now . . . will I someday be Pete's bride?

Epilogue

Three days after Libby's seventeenth birthday, she and Pete were married in an outdoor wedding on the banks of Cherry Creek; Ellie was her maid of honor and caught the bouquet. Libby and Pete had two sons, one who died in infancy, and four daughters. Pete worked at the *Rocky Mountain News* first as a pressman, then as a reporter, and finally as an editor.

Joe studied at Harvard Law School and later became an Idaho State Supreme Court Judge. He married a young woman from Boise, a typesetter for the *Idaho Statesman* newspaper. They had two sons who graduated from Harvard. One became a state senator, but the other joined a traveling circus as a drummer for the band.

Libby's father, Sterling West, became increasingly crippled from his war wounds so he could no longer stand up to set type or run presses at the *Rocky Mountain News*. As a result he became a deskman, skilled at editing copy and mentoring young reporters. His belief that "History is just lies that men have agreed upon" empassioned him to teach journalists that their highest calling is to "Truth and accuracy at all times."

Libby's mother, Julia West, died of cancer in 1887. Sterling died in his sleep four months later.

Ellie Rowe married a prospector from Pikes Peak and settled in Telluride, Colorado. They ran a boarding house that today is a hotel catering to skiers and is operated by two of Ellie's great-granddaughters. Ellie's great-grandson competed in the 1992 Winter Olympics at Albertville, France, in the men's downhill and slalom events.

In 1918 the Spanish Influenza was a worldwide epidemic, killing 30 million people. Libby and Pete were both stricken and died one day apart, having recently celebrated their forty-seventh wedding anniversary. At the time of Libby's death she had written four books of poetry and a novella about a young girl's adventures in a Colorado mining town that was published by a university press.

Exactly 100 years after the transcontinental railroad was completed, Libby's granddaughter, a reporter for the *Los Angeles Times,* wrote about another extraordinary moment in America's history: man's first walk on the moon.

Life in America
in 1868

Historical Note

On May 10, 1869, at Promontory Summit in the territory of Utah, a spike was driven into a railroad tie, changing the history of America. This moment linked the East and West with a transcontinental railroad, one of the most important events in the history of western expansion.

For most people moving west, the vision of plenty of land for farm and family outweighed the fear of life on the "Great American Desert," as the Great Plains were sometimes called. While there were hardly any trees and not enough water, the soil was extremely rich. Usually, boys labored in the fields with their fathers, while girls were assigned tasks indoors. But depending on where help was needed, sometimes girls and their mothers did heavy farmwork, and boys and their fathers washed clothes and worked in the kitchen. But hard work, extreme temperatures, tornadoes, droughts, and the loneliness of the frontier could not deter families searching for the American dream.

The earliest transportation to the West was provided by

flatboats on the Missouri River and its tributaries, but most pioneers and supplies traveled west by wagon train. The largest wagons, pulled by a team of 12 oxen, could carry as much as 5,000 pounds of cargo. The wagons traveled only 15 miles a day, were often preyed upon by robbers, and were not very profitable because of the overhead costs of paying herders, drivers, and providing food for the oxen.

Some people believed that only a transcontinental railroad could truly unite the United States. Rather than a month-long journey by rail and stagecoach, or a five-month-long trip by wagon train, the railroad could go cross-country in six or seven days. Building the railroad was a formidable task, however, and many resisted it.

After years of talk, the Pacific Railroad Act of 1862 was signed on July 1 by President Abraham Lincoln. It authorized the formation of the Union Pacific Railroad, which would build west of the Missouri River to the California border, or wherever it met the tracks of the Central Pacific Railroad which had been formed on June 28, 1861. In the Act, the government agreed to pay the Union and Central Pacific Railroads a certain amount of money per mile of track laid, depending on the difficulty of the terrain: $16,000 east of the Rockies and west of the Sierras; $32,000 between the Rockies and Sierras; and $48,000 in the mountains. In addition, with each mile of track laid, ten square miles of land were granted: five on each side of the tracks in alternating sections, resulting in a checkerboard pattern. The Pacific Railroad Act did not, however, designate a meeting place for the two railroads.

The Central Pacific started laying track in January of 1863, but the Civil War slowed its progress. Investors found that they could make more money from the war, and the army had priority for needed supplies. Further, the Central Pacific had difficulty finding workers because so many men in California went to the gold fields in hopes of striking it rich. James H. Strobridge, the construction boss, hired 50 Chinese men on a trial basis. The Chinese proved that they were just as good, if not better, than the other workers, who were mostly Irish immigrants. Eventually, thousands more Chinese men left their families behind to come to California.

The Central Pacific's rival, the Union Pacific, broke ground on December 2, 1863. However, construction was halted because of lack of funds. Finally, on July 2, 1864, the second Pacific Railroad Act was signed by President Lincoln, increasing the amount of money both railroad companies could receive from the government and doubling their land grants. A work train was organized that included everything from workers' accommodations to general stores to blacksmiths' shops. Separate trains brought railroad ties, spikes, and rails from the East. The workers, who were mostly Irish, German, and Italian immigrants, lived in tent cities put up and taken down as the railroad went west. These towns, dubbed "Hell on Wheels," were known for their rough-and-tumble saloons and dance halls and were populated with gamblers, prostitutes, and drifters. They provided workers with little to spend their money on but liquor, gambling, and women, often resulting in drunken brawls, shootings and knifings. But the workers' behavior was tolerated so long as it did not interfere with the railroad's progress.

In October 1866, when the Union Pacific's tracks reached the 100th meridian of longitude (247 miles west of Omaha), diplomats, congressmen, and other wealthy supporters to the Great Pacific Railroad Excursion were invited to the event. Reporters and photographers were hired to cover the event, which included bands, magicians, and even performances and staged battles by Pawnee Indians. The spectacles reinforced people's prejudices against the Indians, portrayed by the media as wild savages who wanted to sabotage the building of the railroad. In reality, the Indians were only trying to protect the land that they believed rightfully belonged to them. They had been promised in a treaty that the land west of the 95th meridian would be their permanent home. When the railroad reached the 100th meridian, they were angered, and soon began to attack the railroad workers — surveyors, graders, even whole section gangs — and the railroad itself, uprooting rails and tearing down telegraph wires. The railroad, and the settlers who came with it, threatened the Indians' land and the buffalo, which the Indians depended on for food and clothing, as well as for their spiritual value.

In 1868, newspapers from eastern cities sent reporters to the forefront of construction, providing anxious readers with coverage of the daily progress of the railroad, which was now increasingly called "The Great Race," and of news associated with the railroad companies. Since little capital and equipment were needed, local newspapers were also established in the violent "Hell on Wheels" towns, some running a daily column called "Last Night's Shootings." Editors were known for writing freely on politics and other newspapers and editors, which sometimes led to personal violence.

In their rush to win "The Great Race," both railroad

companies were responsible for laying some unsafe tracks. Rails laid on frozen ground buckled during the spring thaw. Some bridges were so weak they could hardly bear a train's weight and were swept away in the spring floods. All of this unusable track eventually had to be relaid, at enormous costs. Also, rather than coming to an agreement on where the tracks should meet, the companies continued to grade two roadbeds and at one point laid duplicate track less than 150 feet apart. By April 9, 1869, when President Grant determined Promontory Summit as the meeting place, the Union and Central Pacific railroads had earned $32,000 per mile for over 290 miles of unnecessary track.

On May 7, 1969, Leland Stanford arrived at Promontory Summit to attend the Golden Spike ceremony. The heads of the Union Pacific, however, were delayed twice: once by angry workers who took them hostage, demanding back pay, and once by rains that weakened a bridge at Devil's Gate. They finally reached their destination late on Sunday, May 9. At noon the next day, the ceremonies commenced. But the "golden spike" that was to join the two sides of the railroad was not golden at all: the gold, silver, and bronze spikes that were initially dropped into place were discreetly removed and replaced with ordinary iron spikes. When Stanford swung the hammer to bang the last spike into place, he missed. Thomas Durant of the Union Pacific stepped up for his turn, but he, too, missed the spike! Fittingly, it was a regular rail worker — one who had probably driven thousands of spikes in his work on the railroad — who drove the last spike and ended the race. Six years after ground was broken, the rails were joined, enabling the Central Pacific's locomotive *Jupiter* and Union Pacific's *No. 119* to at last meet nose to nose.

With the completion of the transcontinental railroad, settlers poured into the West, supporting a booming economy. Along with produce from the thriving farms, resources from the mountains of the West, such as low-grade silver, lead, and copper ores, were shipped to the eastern industrial centers. In turn, eastern companies shipped supplies to the growing western market. Agriculture in the West benefited from farm equipment, technology, new livestock strains, and machinery brought in by rail. Soon financiers built factories in the West. Just as commerce and people traveled by railroad, so did eastern ideas and ways, changing life in the West forever. Only 20 years after the Union and Pacific Railroads were linked, the frontier was a thing of the past.

Sewing by hand was a necessary skill for girls living in the rugged West. It provided an inexpensive way for them to make and mend their own clothes and other useful household items, such as curtains and quilts.

During the 1860s girls wore ruffled bloomers underneath long plaid dresses trimmed with piping. Pictured here are a group of young women playing croquet in Sacramento, California, during the time of the Golden Spike.

Published in 1868, Little Women *by Louisa May Alcott was very popular among young girls, as it still is today. This frontispiece, sketched by Alcott's sister May, appeared in the first volume.*

This front-page advertisement placed in the Rocky Mountain News *on May 11, 1869, features the Home Washing Machine. The ad claimed that this machine could "wash 500 collars and 50 shirts in one hour." Traditionally, washing clothes took place in large pots of boiling water, which took considerably longer.*

Railroad workers and newspaper reporters traveled along the Central Pacific and Union Pacific construction routes. To keep on the move, they used tents for lodging. Dinner on the road usually consisted of meat cooked on a spit, or pointed rod, over an open fire.

The interior of the Laramie Hotel in Laramie, Wyoming, was quite lavish. It provided a welcome change for reporters and their families who had been camping out in the rough Western terrain.

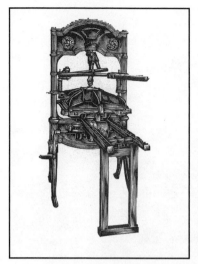

The Washington Hand Press was used to print newspapers. It stood on sturdy iron legs, was about two feet tall, and weighed approximately 700 pounds. Two men were necessary to work the press by hand: one to insert ink and one to move the levers. It could print up to 250 sheets of type in one hour.

Newspapers were briskly set up in tents so that even before towns were established, reporters could cover the building of the railroad. Newspaper workers were known as "stringers" because of the string-like telegraph wire by which they sent their eyewitness reports back to the printing office. Even the smallest settlements often had their own newspapers.

Boundless, craggy wilderness separated the West Coast from the midwestern plains. Rugged mountains, rivers, and miles of desert made the construction of the transcontinental railroad dangerous and costly.

The Union Pacific Railroad Company had approximately 10,000 workers, and tracklaying was extremely organized. Five men would gather on each side of a 500-pound rail and lower it into position. Spikers would then hammer in iron spikes to secure it to the ground. Workers laid at least one mile of track daily, and sometimes as many as eight.

Nearly 2,000 Chinese men helped build the Central Pacific Railroad. This drawing depicts the Chinese laborers in cliff-hanger baskets (like those used in China) at the treacherous Cape Horn peak of the Sierra Nevada range. Dangling a thousand feet in the air, they drilled the rock and blasted it with explosives. This was dangerous work and, sadly, many of the men lost their lives.

The Secrettown Trestle located in California was built by Chinese laborers and was the largest curved trestle at the time. Trestles—frameworks supporting bridges—were necessary to maneuver the railroad tracks through the erratic topography of the West.

Some towns originated as "camps," with small canvas and board shacks serving as stores, hotels, and saloons. Promontory Summit, Utah, (shown here) was the location of the driving of the golden spike when the Central Pacific and Union Pacific Railroads met. Many of the one-street towns out west, like Promontory Summit, prospered briefly and then disappeared.

Engine No. 23 is shown at a railroad stop, fifteen miles west of Laramie, Wyoming. The famous antlers are positioned just above the headlight.

The Central Pacific locomotive Jupiter *(left) and the Union Pacific engine No. 119 (right) met after the last spike was driven at Promontory Summit, Utah, on May 10, 1869. Shaking hands in the center are Chief Engineers Samuel S. Montague (left) of the Central Pacific and Grenville M. Dodge (right) of the Union Pacific, during the Golden Spike ceremony.*

I've been working on the railroad
All the live long day

I've been working on the railroad
to pass the time a-way

Don't you hear the whistle blow-in'
rise up early in the morn
Don't you hear the captain shouting

Di-nah blow your horn
Di-nah, won't you blow,
Di-nah, won't you blow
Di-nah won't you blow your
hor-or-orn?

Di-nah, won't you blow,
Di-nah, won't you blow
Di-nah, won't you blow
your horn?

"I've Been Working on the Railroad" was a favorite song of the railroad workers in the late 1800s.

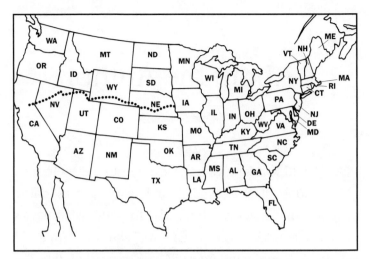

This modern map of the continental United States shows the transcontinental railroad route.

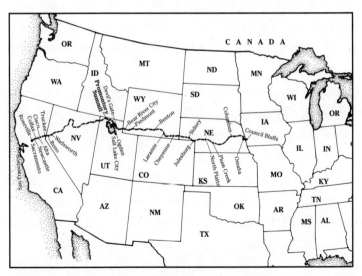

This detail of the transcontinental railroad route shows important stations as well as Promontory Summit, Utah, where the two railroads met.

About the Author

As a child Kristiana Gregory loved history even though in school all she remembered learning was dates, names, and places. "I hungered to know what it was *really* like back in the 'olden days,'" she says. "What did kids think about and how did they spend their time?"

While living in Salt Lake City, Utah, Gregory's apartment was a short walk from Brigham Young's house and other historic buildings and sites, which she often visited. History came alive for her. Thus, when given the opportunity to write about a young girl traveling through Utah alongside builders of the transcontinental railroad, Gregory was thrilled. "It was a chance to journey back in time and imagine life through the eyes of Libby West."

Kristiana Gregory is the author of two previous titles in the Dear America series, both named NCSS-CBC Notable Children's Trade Books in the Field of Social Studies, *The Winter of Red Snow: The Revolutionary War Diary of Abigail Jane Stewart,* an *American Bookseller*

"Pick of the Lists," and *Across the Wide and Lonesome Prairie: The Oregon Trail Diary of Hattie Campbell.* Gregory's other titles with Scholastic are *Jimmy Spoon and the Pony Express, Orphan Runaways,* and *The Stowaway,* which *Parents* magazine named one of their "Best of 1995." She is also author of *Jenny of the Tetons,* winner of the SCBWI Golden Kite Award; *The Legend of Jimmy Spoon;* and *Earthquake at Dawn,* an ALA Best Book for Young Adults. She lives in Idaho with her family.

Acknowledgments

My heartfelt thanks to the rangers of the Golden Spike National Historic Site at Promontory, Utah: Robert Chugg and Bruce Powell for patiently answering questions and helping with research; Robert Hanover for combing through this manuscript, checking historical details, and correcting my errors. Much thanks also to Diane Garvey Nesin for more fact-checking; and to Dick Braese, Curator of Printing Arts at Idaho Historical Museum in Boise, for demonstrating the Washington Hand Printing Press and the old art of setting type by hand. I'm honored by their enthusiasm and willingness to help.

I especially cherish my teenage sons, Greg and Cody Rutty, for being critical listeners to the manuscript-in-progress, and for their tolerance and good humor during our long family trip to Promontory.

Grateful acknowledgment is made for permission to reprint the following:

Cover portrait: *Idle Thoughts* (Petite Fille Assise Brodant) by Adolphe William Bougereau, signed and dated 1903. Oil on canvas, 50⅝ x 26 in. (127.9 x 66 cm). Christie's Images, a division of Christie's Inc., Long Island City, New York

Cover background: *American Railroad Scene: Snowbound.* Lithograph from Currier & Ives. Museum of the City of New York, courtesy of the Harry T. Peters Collection

Page 190 (top): *A Tranquil Hour,* Culver Pictures, New York, New York
Page 190 (bottom): Sacramento maidens playing croquet, Union Pacific Museum Collection, Omaha, Nebraska

Page 191 (top): *Little Women* frontispiece drawing by May Alcott, Culver Pictures, New York, New York

Page 191 (bottom): *Rocky Mountain News* May 11, 1869 advertisement, Denver Public Library, Western History Department, Denver, Colorado

Page 192 (top): Campsite and train of Central Pacific Railroad, photograph by Alfred A. Hart, National Archives

Page 192 (bottom): Interior of Laramie Hotel, photograph by Andrew J. Russell, Union Pacific Museum Collection, Omaha, Nebraska

Page 193 (top): Washington Hand Press, wood engraving by Jon de Pol, *American Iron Hand Presses* by Stephen O. Saxe, Oak Knoll Books

Page 193 (bottom): *Daily Reporter,* Library of Congress

Page 194 (top): Green River Bridge and Citadel Rock, 1868, photograph by Andrew J. Russell, Union Pacific Museum Collection, Omaha, Nebraska

Page 194 (bottom): Laying of the rails of the Union Pacific Railroad, photograph by J. Carbott, ibid.

Page 195: Chinese workers of the Central Pacific Railroad, Kem Lee Studio, courtesy of Kan's Restaurant, San Francisco, taken from *Full Steam Ahead: The Building of the Transcontinental Railroad* by Rhoda Blumberg, National Geographic Society, Washington, D.C.

Page 196 (top): Secrettown Trestle, National Park Service, Department of the Interior

Page 196 (bottom): Promontory Utah, Union Pacific Museum Collection, Omaha, Nebraska

Page 197 (top): Wyoming Station, Engine *No. 23* on main track, photograph by Andrew J. Russell, ibid.

Page 197 (bottom): Joining of the Central Pacific and Union Pacific railroads, ibid.

Page 198: Words and music to "I've Been Working on the Railroad," *The American Song Treasury: 100 Favorites* by Theodore Raph, Dover Publications, New York, New York

Page 199: Maps by Heather Saunders

Other books in the Dear America series

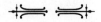

A Journey to the New World
The Diary of Remember Patience Whipple
by Kathryn Lasky

The Winter of Red Snow
The Revolutionary War Diary of Abigail Jane Stewart
by Kristiana Gregory

When Will This Cruel War Be Over?
The Civil War Diary of Emma Simpson
by Barry Denenberg

A Picture of Freedom
The Diary of Clotee, a Slave Girl
by Patricia C. McKissack

Across the Wide and Lonesome Prairie
The Oregon Trail Diary of Hattie Campbell
by Kristiana Gregory

So Far from Home
The Diary of Mary Driscoll, an Irish Mill Girl
by Barry Denenberg

I Thought My Soul Would Rise and Fly
The Diary of Patsy, a Freed Girl
by Joyce Hansen

West to a Land of Plenty
The Diary of Teresa Angelino Viscardi
by Jim Murphy

Dreams in the Golden Country
The Diary of Zipporah Feldman, a Jewish Immigrant Girl
by Kathryn Lasky

A Line in the Sand
The Alamo Diary of Lucinda Lawrence
by Sherry Garland

Standing in the Light
The Captive Diary of Catharine Carey Logan
by Mary Pope Osborne

Voyage on the Great Titanic
The Diary of Margaret Ann Brady
by Ellen Emerson White

My Heart Is on the Ground
The Diary of Nannie Little Rose, a Sioux Girl
by Ann Rinaldi

This book is dedicated with love to my mother,
Jeanne Kern Gregory, my first editor, whose early insistence on good
spelling and good grammar helped me put words on the page.

Copyright © 1999 by Kristiana Gregory

+═══ ═══+

All rights reserved. Published by Scholastic Inc.
555 Broadway, New York, New York 10012.
DEAR AMERICA and the DEAR AMERICA logo are trademarks of Scholastic Inc.

Library of Congress Cataloging-in-Publication Data
Gregory, Kristiana.
The great railroad race : the diary of Libby West / Kristiana Gregory.
p. cm. — (Dear America)
Summary: As the daughter of a newspaper reporter, fourteen-year-old Libby
keeps a diary account of the exciting events surrounding her during the
building of the railroad in the West in 1868.
ISBN 0-590-10991-X
[1. Frontier and pioneer life — West (U.S.) — Fiction.
2. West (U.S.) — Fiction.   3. Diaries — Fiction.]   I. Title.   II. Series.
PZ7.G8619Gr 1999
[Fic] — dc21   98-21816
CIP AC
10 9 8 7 6 5 4 3   9/9 0/0 01 02 03 04

The text type in this book was set in Cheltenham Light.
The display type was set in Edwardian Medium.
Book design by Elizabeth B. Parisi

Printed in the U.S.A.   23
First edition, April 1999

+═══ ═══+